DELTORA QUEST 2

The Isle of Illusion

DELORA QUEST 2

DELTORA QUEST 2

The Isle of Illusion

Emily Rodda

A Scholastic Press
book
from
Scholastic Australia

Scholastic Press
345 Pacific Highway
Lindfield NSW 2070
an imprint of Scholastic Australia Pty Limited (ABN 11 000 614 577)
PO Box 579, Gosford NSW 2250.
www.scholastic.com.au

Part of the Scholastic Group
Sydney ● Auckland ● New York ● Toronto ● London ● Mexico City
● New Delhi ● Hong Kong ● Buenos Aires

First published in 2002.
Text and graphics copyright © Emily Rodda, 2002.
Graphics by Bob Ryan.
Cover illustrations copyright © Scholastic Australia, 2002.
Cover illustrations by Marc McBride.

National Library of Australia Cataloguing-in-Publication entry
Rodda, Emily, 1948–.
    The Isle of illusion.
    ISBN 1 86504 425 3.
    I. Title. (Series: Rodda, Emily, 1948– Deltora quest 2; 2).
A823.3

Typeset in Palatino.

Printed by McPherson's Printing Group, Maryborough Vic.

10 9 8 7 6 5 4 3 2 1   2 3 4 5 / 0

CONTENTS

The story so far . . .

Lief, Barda and Jasmine have learned that the Shadowlands was in ancient times the magical land of Pirra, a beautiful country protected by the fabled Pirran Pipe.

When the Pipe was divided into three parts by the warring Pirran tribes of Plume, Auron and Keras, the Shadow Lord invaded Pirra and the tribes were forced to flee to separate islands in a secret sea below Deltora. The companions are sure that the magic of the Pirran Pipe is the only thing that can help them free the Deltoran slaves in the Shadowlands.

On the island of Plume, they gained the first part of the Pipe. Now they are moving on through the underground sea, seeking the island of Auron.

1 - The Rainbow Sea

Lief and Barda were silent as they paddled the frail boat through the world below the world. Jasmine sat in the front of the boat with Filli on her shoulder. Her eyes were fixed on Kree, who was flying ahead. In her hand was the tiny map that was their only guide to their next goal—the island of Auron.

Above their heads the soaring roof of the great cavern shimmered with opal light. The rippling water surrounding them was like liquid rainbows.

'To think that this wonder exists below Deltora!' Barda murmured, finding his voice at last. 'I still cannot quite believe it.'

'Nor I,' said Lief. 'The caverns of the Plumes—the gold, and the scarlet—were beautiful enough. But this place . . .'

Jasmine moved restlessly. 'Beauty is all very well,' she muttered. 'But we do not know where we are!'

She held up the battered map. 'Ranesh said he

would trust Doran the Dragonlover's maps with his life. But there are no landmarks drawn here. Just four islands, a dotted line which could mean anything, and a few cavern walls.'

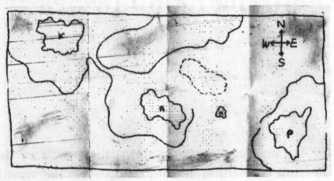

Lief stared at the map, remembering the excitement with which he had traced it in the palace library in Del.

Little had he dreamed then that the Pirran Islands were not in the open sea, but hidden beneath Deltora itself. Little had he dreamed that a short journey to the Os-Mine Hills in pursuit of Jasmine was to lead him into this far longer and more dangerous quest.

With a pang, he thought of home. His long absence must be causing great anxiety. Not for most of the people, who believed their king was still safe in Tora. But for those few who knew he was not.

Doom. His mother. The old librarian, Josef. Josef's assistant, Ranesh. And the girl Marilen.

Most of all, Marilen. What must she be feeling now? Frightened? Lonely? Bitterly regretting that she had ever agreed to leave Tora?

Doom had promised her father that she would be closely guarded. But spies, traitors and assassins were everywhere, as Lief himself knew only too well.

Into his mind came the memory of the first attempts on his life. Both were in the great entrance hall. First, a frenzied, babbling woman had tried to strike him down with a knife. When her attack had failed, she had turned the knife upon herself and died without giving any reason for what she had done.

Not long afterwards, a man who could only walk with the aid of crutches—a man called Moss, a trusted palace guard before the time of the Shadow Lord, Barda said—had seized Lief by the throat as Lief bent over the blanket where he lay.

The choking grip was like iron. It had taken three guards to break it. And then, as Moss was being taken away, someone in the jostling crowd had stabbed him in the back. That person had never been found.

After that, Lief had kept away from crowds. But he had learned that nowhere in the palace was truly safe. Even his own bed chamber.

And why? Why? Lief thought, as he had thought a thousand times before. Why would any Deltoran act as a servant of the Shadow Lord?

Impatiently, he pulled his mind back to the present. 'Doran could not draw landmarks if none existed, Jasmine,' Barda was saying, lifting his paddle from the water and stretching his aching back.

'Do not wake Fury,' Jasmine warned.

Barda glanced quickly at the cage hanging from his belt. But Fury the fighting spider had not moved.

'It is more important not to wake Flash.' Lief nodded at the second cage, resting in the bottom of the boat. 'Flash was the loser in their last battle. He is the one who thirsts for revenge.'

'We are fortunate that the movement of the boat lulls them to sleep,' said Jasmine.

'Indeed, for nothing else does,' Barda growled. 'If only we could have left them behind! This boat is cramped enough without giving room to caged spiders.'

'I do not blame the Plumes for refusing to keep them,' said Jasmine. 'Who would want two beasts who think of nothing but fighting one another?'

Filli snuffled agreement. The huge spiders made him nervous.

They fell silent once more, gazing around them.

Unbroken water met their eyes on every side. The cavern wall through which they had passed to reach this glittering sea was lost in the hazy distance. There was no sign of another.

'At least we know where we are in Deltora,' said Lief at last. 'When we first went underground in the Os-Mine hills, the cavern walls and roof shone gold like the topaz, the Del tribe's talisman. But by the time we reached the island of Plume, the cavern walls were shining red.'

'So we can guess that Plume lies below Deltora's north-east—the land of the Ralad people, whose talisman is the ruby,' said Barda.

Lief nodded. 'And now we are in the territory of the opal. We must be moving west, beneath the Plains. And the island of Auron is near, I am sure of it.'

He broke off as sweet, piping music filled his mind—the music of the Pirran Pipe, calling to him through time. The sound had come to him before, but it was more compelling now. Because now he possessed the mouthpiece of the Pipe itself.

The mouthpiece hung around his neck. It was muffled in a red cloth bag and hidden beneath his clothes. Yet he could feel its power, as once he had felt the magic of the Belt of Deltora.

He could feel, too, its yearning to be joined once more with the other two parts of the Pipe, from which it had been separated so long ago.

'Lief! Barda!'

Lief jumped slightly as Jasmine's voice broke the spell of the music. He saw that she was holding out her arm to Kree, who was swooping towards her.

'Kree sees land ahead!' Jasmine called excitedly. 'Land!'

Land . . . Land . . . Land . . . murmured the echoes.

Lief's heart beat faster as he and Barda plunged their paddles into the rainbow water and the boat began moving forward once more.

✦

Far away, in the palace in Del, Josef the librarian sighed. The day was still young, but comparing the official library catalogue to the books actually on the shelves was a sad and tiring task.

Many books were missing. Some might have been put away on the wrong shelves. But most, Josef suspected, had been quietly removed and destroyed, because they contained things that the Shadow Lord had wanted Deltorans to forget.

At least I was able to save *The Deltora Annals*, Josef thought, glancing at the pale blue books standing in pride of place near the library work tables. So King Lief was able to read of the Pirran Pipe, the only thing which can help him save the prisoners in the Shadowlands. And he could see Doran's map, which will lead him to the three parts of the Pipe when he returns from the Os-Mine Hills.

When he returns . . . Josef's brow creased. Now he came to think about it, where *was* Lief? Surely he should have returned long ago.

The old librarian's stomach knotted with sudden fear. Why, Lief and the Belt of Deltora were the land's only defences against the Shadow Lord. What if . . . ?

Ringing laughter disturbed the library's silence. Startled and angered, Josef shuffled forward, but stopped when he saw where the sound was coming from.

His apprentice, Ranesh, was bending over the table where sat Marilen, the young Toran visitor who had spent many hours in the library of late.

Marilen had several weighty books open in front

of her, but she was looking up at Ranesh, her eyes dancing. As Josef watched, Ranesh murmured something, and the girl laughed again.

Josef hesitated, very troubled. He was not wise in the ways of the world, but he had been young once. Something about that laughter, and the look on Marilen's face, warned him that this situation was not as it should be.

Lief had asked Josef to make Marilen welcome in the library, but not to speak of her to others. Marilen was a very special guest, Lief had said, but her presence in the palace must be kept secret—at least until his return from the Os-Mine Hills.

Josef had smiled discreetly. He had not been in the palace long, but already he had heard the rumours that Lief had gone to Tora to choose a bride. He had no doubt as to who this beautiful, high-born young lady called Marilen was.

Now this same young lady was laughing with Ranesh in a way that did not seem at all fitting. And Ranesh was surely leaning far too close to one who was the future queen of Deltora.

Josef felt panic rise within him. Nothing but harm could come of this. Harm for the girl who had been put in his care. And terrible harm to Ranesh, who Josef loved liked the son he had never had.

Bitterly Josef blamed himself for being so wrapped up in his work that he had failed to see what was happening under his very nose. He had paid no attention to how much time the two young people were spending together.

I must stop this at once, before it goes too far! he thought wildly. I must speak to Ranesh. Send him away, perhaps. Just for a time. Until—

At that moment, Ranesh looked up and his eyes met Josef's. His teeth flashed in a seemingly casual grin. But Josef knew his apprentice too well to be deceived. Josef recognised the gleam in those dark eyes.

It was the gleam of defiance. Josef remembered it from the days of the Shadow Lord's rule, when Ranesh had often slipped back into their cellar home below the old pottery with bread, cheese or fruit under his jacket.

Josef, weak with hunger, had always eaten what he was given. But he had felt uneasy, nonetheless. He knew that Ranesh, once a homeless orphan surviving alone on the streets of Del, would not hesitate to steal to feed them both.

'Did we disturb you, Josef?' Ranesh called. 'I am sorry. But Marilen and I have just discovered that we are both from the west. She is from Tora, I from Where Waters Meet. Is it not strange?'

'I am going down to the kitchen for a warming drink, Ranesh,' Josef said stiffly. 'Please join me as soon as you can. I wish to talk to you about—about an important matter.'

He turned abruptly and hobbled out of the library. Nodding to the guards, he started moving carefully down the stairs.

Josef had never felt less like a warming drink. His fears had made him far too warm already. But he knew that the kitchen would be a safe place to talk to Ranesh, for Marilen never ventured below the library floor. Her meals were all carried up to her bed chamber by Sharn, Lief's mother.

It is a lonely life for a young girl, Josef thought. No wonder she enjoys Ranesh's company. And he must be flattered and pleased by the admiration of one so beautiful and high-born. But it will not do. No, it will not do.

Clinging tightly to the banisters, he began to move a little faster. Oh, let Lief be safe, and let him return soon, he thought desperately. Then there will be no need for me to send Ranesh away. Lief's return will solve everything!

2 - Warnings

Little knowing the trouble that was brewing in Del—more trouble than even Josef suspected—Lief was paddling as fast as he could towards the land ahead.

The island was shimmering in the distance. Bright pink and yellow weed grew thickly in the shallows that surrounded it. Several times Lief thought he glimpsed movement on the shore, but it was difficult to be sure.

'I can see small buildings, I think,' said Jasmine, squinting into the rainbow haze. 'Not like the houses of the Plumes, though. Much simpler dwellings, shaped like cones. Of course, they could be rocks . . .'

'Indeed they could, and probably are,' Barda growled. 'If the map is accurate, and our course has been straight, this land is not Auron, but the small island to its east. The one marked with a cross.'

'We should keep our wits about us, in any case,' said Jasmine. 'Remember what Clef and Azan said.'

Lief remembered only too well. The people of

Plume had given their part of the Pirran Pipe gladly. But they had warned the companions that the people of Auron would not do the same with the Pipe's stem.

The Plumes had nothing but hatred for their ancient enemies. They wanted to attack Auron and take the second part of the Pipe by force. Their anger had flared when Lief disagreed.

The Plume leader, the Piper, Nols, had frowned. And the young Plumes, Clef and Azan in particular, had argued violently.

'The people of Auron will use their magic against you without pity!' Clef cried. 'To enter their territory unprotected would be madness! They are as savage as the monsters they breed in their seas.'

'The Aurons *breed* monsters?' Barda exclaimed disbelievingly.

'Indeed! There are many old tales of it,' Clef insisted. 'We have long believed that The Fear, the beast you killed, was sent by the Aurons to prey upon us.'

Azan nodded agreement. 'And they will never give up their part of the Pirran Pipe. Never, while they live. What is more, they will take *our* part of the Pipe from you, and keep it for themselves!'

'No. It will be safe with us,' said Lief steadily.

'Your promises are useless,' cried Azan. 'Once the Aurons see you in one of our boats, they will slay you as viciously as they would slay three defenceless Plumes.'

'We are not defenceless!' Jasmine snapped. 'And

how do you know what the Aurons would do? The way between your sea and theirs has only now been opened after hundreds of years. Their feelings about you may have changed.'

'Why should they?' Clef asked shortly. 'Our feelings about *them* have not changed.'

The arguments had continued for days, but at last the companions had been allowed to leave alone. Plume was far behind them now. Their memories of their friends' warnings had not faded, however. If anything, they had grown stronger.

Lost in his thoughts, Lief jumped as Jasmine jerked back with a hiss, reaching for her dagger.

'What is it?' Barda demanded urgently.

Jasmine pointed. Lief and Barda craned forward, and at last saw what her sharper eyes had seen before them.

A ragged shadow was surging towards them, just below the surface of the gleaming water.

Lief's heart hammered in his chest as he threw down his paddle and drew his sword. The thing streaking towards them was large—large enough to upset the boat. It was closing in with amazing speed, changing shape as it came, great arms spreading . . .

A small, sleek head broke the surface. Then there was another, and another. The next moment, all the companions were laughing with relief.

The shadow they had so feared was not a single beast at all, but a group of small, plump creatures with tiny eyes and long whiskers. The little animals frolicked around the boat, playfully butting one another and making tiny chittering sounds.

They were covered with smooth, silvery-grey fur and had fin-like paddles instead of arms and legs. They seemed to breathe air, but were as at home in the water as any fish.

'The island ahead might be their breeding ground,' said Barda, picking up his paddle again. 'Ah, I long to stretch my legs. I am cramped to death in this boat.'

He looked around. 'Are my eyes playing tricks on me, or has the light dimmed a little?' he asked.

Jasmine lifted her head from her delighted study of the animals. 'I had not noticed, but you are right!' she said, in tones of surprise. 'It is as if a cloud has passed over the sun. But there are no clouds here.'

'The Plumes did warn us that their magic could not light the caverns all the way to Auron,' said Lief.

He felt a chill as the words left his lips. He had assumed that where the Plumes' magic failed, the Aurons' magic would take over.

But what if he had been wrong? What if the light failed altogether?

They moved forward once more. The little grey creatures accompanied them for a time, but as the boat neared land and finally crossed the broad band of pink and yellow weed, they dropped back. The next time Lief looked behind him, they had disappeared.

The island certainly did not look inviting. It was

bare and bleak, its barren clay riddled with holes like a pock-marked face.

The gleaming mud of the narrow shore was rippled with ridges created by the tide. Beyond the shore, on slightly higher ground, were straggling groups of the lumpy, cone-shaped objects Jasmine had seen from afar. They seemed to be made of dried mud, but were surely not big enough to be dwellings.

There was no sign of life at all.

The movement I thought I saw must have been a trick of the light, Lief told himself.

And yet he felt danger. The silence, broken only by the soft lapping of water on mud, seemed heavy with menace.

Jasmine was also uneasy.

'I do not like this place,' she said in a low voice. 'Filli and Kree do not like it either. I do not think we should land after all.'

'I see nothing to fear,' Barda said irritably. He moved his cramped legs restlessly and the toe of his boot overturned Flash's cage. Flash woke, and at once began leaping and plunging, beating against the cage bars.

'Now see what you have done, Barda!' Jasmine scolded. 'Now Fury will wake as well, and we will have no peace.'

'Fury had better not wake, or it will be the worse for her,' growled Barda. 'I am a patient man, but my patience is being sorely tested at present.'

Lief did not want to set foot on the island. But he

wanted a quarrel even less. 'Let us land, just for a few minutes,' he suggested. 'We need not stray far from the water.'

Jasmine glowered at him. 'My injured arm is paining me,' Lief murmured, taking refuge in a small white lie. 'I would be grateful if you could paddle in my place for a time, Jasmine. And it will be safer to change seats on dry land.'

'Why did you not say so before, Lief?' Jasmine demanded. 'Of course we will land, then.'

How tactful I am becoming, Lief said grimly to himself, as he and Barda began paddling once more. I am learning the ways of the palace all too well.

This thought made his mind fly again to home. How he longed to know what was happening there! Had Marilen had word from her father? Was she safe and well?

I cannot know these things! he told himself impatiently. It is useless to fret, and probably needless. As long as no-one knows Marilen is in the palace, or who she is, she will be safe.

He looked up, frowning, and caught Jasmine's eye. He made himself smile, but the grin must have looked forced, for she did not smile back.

Jasmine knows me too well, Lief thought. She senses that my mind is full of things she knows nothing about, and it annoys her. But this is one secret I cannot tell—to anyone.

Looking at Jasmine's closed face, an immense

feeling of loneliness swept over him. He wished with all his heart that the easy companionship they had once shared would return. But he knew that while he had to guard his tongue and his thoughts, this could not be.

In time, I hope, Jasmine and Barda will know all, and surely then they will forgive me for my silence, he thought. Surely they will understand that it was not that I did not trust them. I would trust them both with my life!

They reached the shore and together pulled the boat out of the water. Flash was still raging in his cage, and they decided to leave him where he was. Fury had not yet woken, and for this they were grateful.

Barda stretched his limbs with relief. 'Ah, it is good to be on land again—even such miserable land as this!' He looked around, then began to stride towards the cone-like shapes they had seen from the boat.

'Do not go too far!' Jasmine called after him.

'Do not fear,' Barda shouted back, his temper much improved by freedom from the boat. ' I simply want to look at these cones. They interest me.'

He had only moved a few more paces, however, when he stopped dead. Silently, without turning around, he beckoned. Lief and Jasmine hurried to his side.

'There,' Barda breathed, pointing.

Movement could be seen inside the holes that scarred the bare earth around the cones. As the companions watched, heads began to poke cautiously from the holes—smooth, round heads with huge, blinking eyes and two short, slim tubes where nose and mouth should be.

'What are they?' whispered Lief, fascinated.

'Some sort of worm, or grub, by the look of things,' Barda answered, peering at the holes. 'Ah, yes! They have decided we are safe. They are coming out of hiding.'

Sure enough, the creatures were all slowly easing their way out of their holes. As Barda had guessed, they looked like giant caterpillars, with long, pale bodies divided into plump segments, and six stubby legs that scrabbled in the mud as they crept along.

Filli chattered nervously and Kree squawked.

'They do not look dangerous,' said Jasmine. But she felt for her dagger all the same.

'This may be where the legend of the Auron monsters came from,' Barda murmured. 'Perhaps the Aurons breed these things for food. They are fat enough. And standing upright they would be as tall as Nols, at least.'

As he said this, the creatures nearest to them did in fact raise their bodies from the ground and stand balanced on their back legs. Their front and middle legs waggled comically in the air, their huge eyes blinked short-sightedly.

'We had better leave them to their island,' said Lief. 'We seem to be disturbing them.'

He glanced over his shoulder to see how far away the boat was, and received a shock. More of the giant grubs were rearing up behind him. Their bodies glistened with wet mud. Fresh, oozing holes in the rippled shore showed how they had approached without being seen.

'Barda! Jasmine!' Lief whispered, reaching for his sword.

A grub leaned slightly forward. A jet of bright yellow mist hissed from the tube just below its eyes.

Lief jerked backwards, but too late. The mist was already in his eyes and nose, stinging and burning.

He heard himself crying out in shock and pain, felt himself staggering. There was a moment of flashing, spinning colour.

Then, there was nothing.

3 - Reunion

Had Josef known what was happening to his king, he would have been filled with terror. As it was, by the time he at last entered the palace kitchen, he felt only dread at the thought of his forthcoming talk with Ranesh.

The big, homely room was deserted except for one thin old woman. She was standing at the stove with her back to the door, stirring a great pot of stew. Piles of bowls stood nearby, waiting to be filled for the crowds in the entrance hall. Marilen's tray lay lonely on another counter, already set with napkin, knife and fork.

Dismally, Josef hobbled to the table and sat down to wait for Ranesh.

The old woman did not turn to greet him. This surprised him, for all the people he had met in the palace before this had been very friendly.

He coughed politely, but still the cook made no response.

Have it your own way, then, you cross old dame, thought Josef with irritation. I have more than enough to think about without caring for your conversation.

Just then, the woman put down the spoon and turned from the stove. Catching sight of Josef, she jumped violently and shrieked.

Josef leaped in his seat, almost as startled as she. Then, as she began to laugh with embarrassment at her fright, pressing her hand to her chest to still her racing heart, he received another shock.

He knew this woman! He knew that laughter. Knew that face. It was sadly changed since last he saw it long ago. But beneath the ugly scars that marked the cheeks and brow, and the lines of suffering and grief, it was still a face he had known and loved.

He stumbled to his feet.

'Amarantz!' he cried. 'Why—why, Amarantz of the pottery, it is you! I did not know you!'

The woman stared at him, bewildered, for a moment. Then her eyes widened in amazement.

'Josef!' she exclaimed, with a sob, flinging herself into his arms. 'I never thought to see you again!'

'Nor I you!' Josef babbled, almost overwhelmed by joy. 'How did you escape? What of the others?'

But Amarantz said nothing, and at last Josef drew a little away from her, and looked searchingly into her face. 'Amarantz, why do you not answer?' he asked.

The old woman smiled sadly and shook her head. 'I am sorry, Josef,' she said. 'I see your lips move, but I cannot hear you. I am stone deaf.'

From the pocket of her apron she drew a small slate and a piece of chalk. She pressed them into Josef's hands.

Josef took the chalk and wrote.

DEAF? HOW?

Amarantz shrugged. 'The Grey Guards marched us to the Shadowlands border. I could not move fast enough for their liking. They called me old and useless—said I would slow their way through the mountains. They beat me until I was senseless, and left me to die.'

She touched the scars on her face and her mouth twisted with remembered pain. 'I was tougher than they thought. I survived—but the beating had destroyed my hearing. Not that this mattered to me. I had already lost everything I cared about. I have lived—or existed, rather—wandering in the north ever since. I came back to Del only a few days ago.'

Josef rubbed the slate clean with his sleeve, and wrote again, with unsteady hand.

THE OTHERS?

A shadow seemed to pass over Amarantz's face as she stared at the words. 'The others—my sons, their wives, my grandchildren . . . and our friends in the resistance—' Her lips trembled. 'If they still live, they are slaves in the Shadowlands. Beaten, tormented slaves. You and Ranesh were lucky, Josef.'

Her voice broke, and she bowed her head.

Josef patted her arm awkwardly, filled with helpless grief and pity. Guilt, too, because he and Ranesh had been spared while disaster had fallen on those who had sheltered them.

After a long moment, Amarantz scrubbed at her eyes with her apron and straightened her shoulders. 'I must not give way now,' she murmured. 'I have a mission here, and weakness will not help me.'

Seeing Josef's puzzlement, she lifted her chin. 'Why do you think I made the long, hard journey back to Del after all these years?' she demanded. 'It was because I knew that Sharn would remember me from the old days. Lief, too, perhaps, though he was only a small boy when I used to visit the forge to get shoes for Dolly, our old horse. Do you remember Dolly, Josef?'

Josef nodded, his chest aching with memory.

'I saw Sharn this morning,' Amarantz continued. 'She offered food and money freely, of course, but that was not what I wanted. I begged for work in the palace. I need to be here, though I did not tell her why.'

She lowered her voice. 'I am going to speak to Lief, Josef. Find him alone, and make him understand that he must—he *must*—lead an army of rescue to the Shadowlands, whatever his doubts. The people cry out for it, and he does not listen. But surely he will listen to me! An old friend—who has lost so much.'

Josef stared at her in dismay. But Amarantz did not seem to notice his expression. Her own face had brightened. 'Why, Josef, I remember now,' she cried excitedly. 'You were once the palace librarian! In the north it is said that Lief spends his days in the library. You could take me to him!'

Josef felt desperate. He could not tell Amarantz the truth. But she had to know, at least, that he could not take her to Lief. That Lief was not in the palace.

There is no help for it, he thought. I will have to tell her the lie that everyone else believes.

He took the slate and wrote.

LIEF IS IN TORA

The old woman's eyes opened wide. 'The king has fled to Tora?' she cried. 'I did not hear the news.' Her voice rose to a wail. 'This cursed deafness! I did not know. Tora!'

Aimlessly she turned from the stove and stumbled towards the door that led to the outside air. As Josef watched helplessly, she reached for the doorknob, then let her trembling hand fall.

'What am I thinking? I cannot reach him there,' she mumbled. 'So it was all for nothing. There is no hope. No hope.' She pressed her hands to her face, and began sobbing in an agony of grief.

Josef could not bear it. He hobbled to her side, tapped her arm to gain her attention, and scribbled on the slate.

HE WILL RETURN SOON

'No!' moaned Amarantz. 'He knows that in Tora he will be safe. Why should he return?'

Throwing caution to the winds, Josef wrote again and thrust the slate in front of her streaming eyes.

LIEF MUST RETURN. HIS TORAN BRIDE IS HERE. UPSTAIRS. SECRET. TELL NO ONE.

Amarantz stared, and slowly her terrible sobbing died away. She took a deep, shuddering breath.

But before she could say a word, the door behind her was flung open. An enormous, roughly dressed figure wearing a cap of fur burst into the room, hauling another, much smaller, figure after it.

'Where is Doom?' the tall stranger roared. 'Bring him at once!'

Frantically, Josef wiped his sleeve over the slate, rubbing out the chalked words.

He was shaking, sweating all over.

Who were these people? Had they seen the message on the slate? Was that why they were asking for Doom? To report Josef's treachery? To have him thrown into prison?

'What are you gawping at, old fossil?' roared the giant stranger, tearing off the fur cap to reveal a shaved skull painted with swirling red designs. 'Move your skinny shanks! Tell Doom that Lindal of Broome is here,

24

and that he must see her. At once!'

The stranger was a woman! His head reeling, Josef turned to do as she asked. But at the same moment the door which led to the front of the palace opened a little, and Ranesh's dark, watchful face appeared in the gap.

At the sight of a newcomer, the small stranger held out his hand pathetically. 'Help me, I beg you, kind sir!' he quavered. 'A little food . . . a sip of ale . . .'

Lindal thrust him away from her with a snort of contempt. He squeaked and dropped to the floor, rolling on the stones and moaning piteously.

'I found this puny, whining fellow by the side of the north road,' the giant woman roared. 'He has terrible news of the king!'

Josef's heart seemed to leap into his throat. He saw Ranesh's eyes gleam with sudden fire.

'I tried to save him!' wailed the rolling figure on the floor. 'I fought like a demon till the end. But what could one poor, starving acrobat do against so many Granous? What could poor Jinks do?'

4 - Trapped

While Jinks told lies of him in Del, Lief was struggling in the grip of a terrifying nightmare. He was trapped in a coffin. He was trying to beat at the coffin walls, but his arms and legs would not move. He was trying to open his eyes, but his eyes were sealed. He was trying to scream, but could not make a sound.

Somewhere, Kree was screeching. But closer, much closer, there were other sounds—small slapping, scratching sounds which filled Lief with dread.

Desperately he tried to wake, to free himself from the horror that had engulfed him. But every time he struggled towards consciousness, the dream dragged him down once more.

Then Kree screeched again, and this time the harsh sound was loud—loud enough to jolt Lief into true wakefulness.

He forced his sticky eyes open. He saw the tip of a

black wing as Kree soared upward again, out of his view. And then, with a pang of pure terror, he realised that the dream had been real.

Or almost real. He was not lying in a coffin. He was upright. But his legs were pressed together and his arms were pinned to his sides. He could not move his head. His nose was filled with the smell of mud. His mouth was choked with it.

At first, he did not understand what had happened to him. Then he remembered.

The island, with its rippled shore and strange, cone-shaped rocks. The grub creature leaning forward, huge-eyed. The jet of yellow mist . . .

His bleary eyes focused on a tall cone standing directly in front of him. Giant grubs were crawling all over the cone, moving busily up and down.

Dimly Lief realised that they were building. They were bringing clay from the ground, mixing the clay with liquid that dribbled from their tube-like mouths, and patting the resulting mud onto the sides of the cone.

His gaze moved to the cone's tip and his stomach churned as he glimpsed Barda's head and face, almost covered by a lumpy helmet of thick, dried mud.

One of the grubs was working there. With its stubby front legs it patted and smoothed the sticky clay mess into a gap beside Barda's mouth. It waited for a moment as the mud lightened and hardened with amazing speed. Then it hurried down to the ground again

Lief fought down panic as he realised that he

himself was imprisoned as Barda was. A thick shroud of dried mud encased him from head to toe.

He could still breathe through his nose, and he could still see. But he knew that would not last long. His skin crawled as he heard a scrabbling sound near his ear. Out of the corner of his eye he saw a large-eyed head nod towards him. He felt a horrible wet coolness on his cheek as new mud was pressed into place.

The grub which had been working on Barda's mouth climbed the cone again, crawling over the mass of its fellows, who were adding to a lump of clay near the middle of the cone. Fury's cage, Lief realised.

Small, familiar sounds were coming from beneath the lump. Fury was awake, and raging. The yellow vapour had not affected her. Perhaps it worked only on warm-blooded creatures.

But even a fighting spider cannot live without air for long, Lief thought. Soon Fury will die. Like us.

He realised that Kree had stopped screeching. Had Kree finally accepted that he could not attack the grubs for fear of being stunned by the yellow mist himself? Had he, perhaps, been caught on that last, desperate swoop?

Or—Lief felt a chill run through him—or had Kree sped away in despair because he had seen Jasmine, and Filli with her, smothered in choking mud?

The cones within his view were far too small to contain Jasmine's body. A few had been broken open.

The one standing beside Barda had several holes

in its centre. Through the gaps, silvery grey fur gleamed. Lief guessed that inside the cone was the preserved body of one of the little sea moles the companions had seen further out to sea.

No doubt the moles are the grubs' usual prey, he thought. The herd we met would not follow us to the island, but other herds, no doubt, are not so wise. And the young, the weak, the lost and the injured would often be washed to shore.

A mud grub crawled up to the scarred cone. It lifted its front feet from the ground and grasped the cone firmly. It stuck its mouth tube into one of the gaps in the clay. Its body rippled as it drank.

Lief felt sick. So this was to be their fate. To die sealed within a coffin of clay, and then for months to be a food supply for the grubs. With all his might he tried to flex his arms, move his legs, twist his neck—anything to crack the walls that imprisoned him.

But he could not move a muscle. His legs were pressed too tightly together. His arms were held too firmly by his sides. The grubs had done their work too well.

With a shudder he felt the return of the grub that had been covering his face. He shut his eyes to block out the sight of its bobbing head, its blank stare, as fresh mud was patted onto his cheek, close beside his nose.

Then, suddenly, the patting and smearing stopped, as though the grub had been disturbed in its work.

Lief opened his eyes. The grub had moved out of

sight, leaving its task only half completed.

It was clear that something unusual was happening. The grubs working on Barda's cone were turning their heads, wriggling urgently. And the one feeding on the dead sea mole was pulling abruptly away from its meal, brown liquid dribbling horribly from its mouth tube.

The next moment, the grubs on Barda's cone were scattering in a cloud of yellow vapour. A ferocious, yellow-backed brown spider had hurled itself into their midst, fangs snapping viciously.

Lief stared. Flash! But how could this be? Flash had been trapped in his cage at the bottom of the boat.

Somewhere above, Kree screeched triumphantly.

Lief's heart leaped as he realised what had happened. Kree had opened the cage door. Kree had known that Flash, free at last, would have only one thing in mind: to reach Fury, wherever Fury might be.

Huge as he was, the giant spider seemed small compared to the grubs. But the grubs had no weapon except the yellow mist, which seemed to have no effect on Flash at all. And he had huge fangs, eight spiny legs, enormous strength and a fierce will to win.

Grubs fell writhing to the ground as Flash bit and tore at them, ripping between times at the clay over Fury's cage. Already a few bars of the cage had been exposed, and Fury herself, desperate for air, was throwing herself against them, inflaming Flash even more.

More grubs were streaming into Lief's view every

moment. It looked as if the whole colony was rushing to defend the cone in which Barda was trapped. The cone's lower half was covered in a seething mass of bodies. Flash was wreathed in swirling yellow mist as the newcomers attacked her in the only way they knew.

It is fortunate that the mist is not rising, or Barda would be unconscious again in a moment, Lief thought. Then all Flash's work would be of no use.

But would it be of use in any case? The widening hole around Fury's cage would not help Barda break out of his prison. The hardened clay around the big man's arms and legs was untouched.

Then Lief felt something. The clay that cloaked his own left hand was being tapped strongly by something hard and sharp.

Lief guessed what it was, but did not let himself believe it until Kree's beak broke through the clay and stabbed his wrist.

Never had Lief felt pain so joyously.

Another two taps and the clay covering his hand had cracked away completely. Violently Lief scrabbled at the edges of the hole, making it larger. Then, as Kree began work on his other hand, Lief felt even more vibrations—a scratching and scraping near his foot.

'Lief!'

With wild joy, Lief recognised the whispering voice. Jasmine was crouching by his right side. He could not see her, but he could feel her dagger chipping at the hard shell that imprisoned him.

Jasmine was alive! Kree must have rushed to free her as soon as the grubs left her to defend Barda's cone.

'As soon as you feel my dagger against your boot, begin to kick,' Jasmine whispered. 'We may not have much time.'

Lief felt movement near his chin and, squinting downward, saw a small grey shape. His fur spiked with mud, Filli was nibbling and clawing furiously at the clay that swathed Lief's neck.

Lief felt the point of Jasmine's dagger against his foot and began kicking towards it, feeling clay crumbling away. He felt her start work on the other side. He felt clay crack from his right hand and wrist as Kree's sharp beak broke through.

His left arm was already free to the elbow. He could bend it. And, thanks to Filli, he could move his head from side to side once more.

He struggled desperately, his eyes fixed on the squirming mass of grubs at the base of Barda's cone. Absorbed by their struggle with Flash, the grubs still had not noticed what was happening behind their backs.

But at any moment, surely, one of them would turn and give the alarm. Then all would be lost.

Lief closed his eyes and took a deep breath, summoning up all his strength. He imagined the clay as an egg, enclosing him. Then, with every muscle in his body, he pushed outward, willing the shell to crack.

5 - Hopes and Fears

There was a long moment of tension. Then, suddenly, the clay shell simply shattered, falling in great chunks to the ground.

The grubs at the base of Barda's cone turned, huge blank eyes staring. They remained absolutely still for a single moment, then reared up, twisting and turning, heads bobbing. Some began scrambling rapidly towards Lief.

Lief staggered, off-balance. His left foot was still trapped. He kicked violently, fumbling for his sword.

'Lief! Cover your face! They will try to spray you again!' he heard Jasmine shout.

Lief glanced around, sword in hand. Jasmine, her mouth and nose covered by a scarf, was scooping Filli from the rubble. Covered in clay dust, chattering frantically, Filli leaped to her shoulder and dived under her collar.

Then Jasmine was darting away without a

33

backward glance, lunging towards Barda. Three grubs reared up, blocking her path. She dodged aside, covering her muffled face. The grubs sprayed yellow mist after her, but did not attempt to give chase.

The grubs approaching Lief had also stopped. It seemed to have been decided between them that all their energies should be devoted to protecting Barda, their remaining, and finest, prize.

With his free hand, Lief snatched at the hem of his cloak and dragged it up, winding the cloth around his face so that its dusty folds covered his nose. He kicked away the last of the clay and staggered forward.

Flash was taking no notice of the panic around her. She had completely uncovered Fury's cage now, and the two spiders were trying to fight through the bars. The cage was swinging violently, chipping away more clay every moment. Lief could clearly see Barda's jacket, his belt buckle—even the hilt of his sword.

The grubs had stopped trying to mend the gap. Now they were concentrating on Barda's face, no doubt aware that the sooner he was dead, the sooner they would be left in peace.

Barda's eyes were open. He was staring straight at Lief.

Lief knew what those eyes were saying.

Leave me. Take the boat and go. You cannot help me.

Lief shook his head violently. He took another step.

Too close. A grub reared up at him. He jumped away, pressing his cloak hard against his face to avoid the burst of spray that would make him a prisoner once more.

Dagger in hand, Jasmine was warily circling Barda's cone, keeping a good distance from the thrashing grubs that guarded it. Lief ran to her side.

'Kree and I cannot get near him, Lief,' Jasmine muttered. 'They spray as soon as we try. If only we had a tool with a very long handle. Then, perhaps, we could smash the clay from a distance. But we brought nothing like that with us, and the boat's paddles are far too short and frail to be of use.'

Lief ran over the contents of the boat in his mind and reluctantly decided that Jasmine was right. There was nothing of use in the boat. Nothing but food, water, sleeping blankets, baling buckets, rope . . .

Buckets! Rope! An idea struck him like a bolt of lightning.

'There is another way to break the clay,' he said, gripping Jasmine's arm. 'Come with me.'

He told her his plan as they raced to the boat. They snatched up a coil of rope, and the buckets used for baling. They filled the buckets with water, hurried back to the place where Barda stood, and dashed the water onto the base of the cone.

The grubs there reared and hissed, but did not retreat. Flash and Fury, their hard, spiny bodies wet and glistening, fought on as if nothing had happened. The water streamed off the hardened clay and sank quickly into the softer earth beneath.

'Quickly!' Lief gave Jasmine one end of the rope, keeping the other end in his own hand. They set off rapidly in opposite directions, their arms held high, circling the cone once, twice, like children playing a game. Loops of rope tightened around the cone, just above Fury's cage. Confused, the grubs hissed at the loops, and began running up and down, trying to cover them with clay.

Jasmine and Lief came together on the shore behind the cone.

'Now!' Lief breathed. And pulled his end of the rope with all his strength.

He heard Jasmine groaning with effort as she, too, heaved with all her might. He heard the blood pounding in his ears. He heard Kree screeching above his head.

And then, at last, he heard the sound he had been waiting for—a sucking, squelching sound, as the soggy earth beneath the cone released its hold. Slowly, the cone began to tilt towards him.

He shouted in triumph, and heard Jasmine's voice joining his own as together they ploughed backwards, the lines of rope straining between the cone and their aching hands.

Then, quite suddenly, the cone was toppling. The grubs were scattering in confusion and panic. And Lief and Jasmine were staggering back, falling, sprawling, as the cone fell crashing to the ground.

Lief scrambled to his feet. Dust hung in a low cloud above the ruins of Barda's prison and the bodies of crushed and dying grubs. Barda himself lay groaning amidst the rubble. Rearing and twisting frantically, the surviving grubs were coming out of hiding and hurrying towards him, yellow vapour already puffing from the tubes below their eyes.

Lief and Jasmine ran to Barda and dragged him to his feet. Dazed, confused, he stumbled between them towards the boat.

Lief saw, to his amazement, that Flash was still clinging to the cage attached to Barda's belt. Covered in dust, almost as dazed as Barda himself, the spider had stopped fighting with Fury, and was hunched like a bundle of sticks against the cage bars.

'Make haste!' Jasmine urged, glancing behind her.

Lief looked over his shoulder in turn and saw that the grubs had disappeared from sight. But the area around the patch of rubble was pitted with holes. The beasts were tunnelling towards them.

The companions reached the boat and Lief and Jasmine hauled it down to the waterline. All around them the wet mud was beginning to bubble as grubs came to the surface.

'In! In!' shrieked Jasmine, pushing at Barda feverishly. He tumbled into the boat and lay there mumbling and groaning as his companions splashed into the muddy water, hauling the boat behind them.

In seconds, pale heads began emerging from the sand. But Lief and Jasmine were already scrambling into their craft and taking up the paddles. They were paddling furiously away, into ever deeper water.

Only when they had crossed the band of bright seaweed that ringed the island did they look back. The shore they had left behind them was squirming with grubs and veiled in a thick yellow haze. And in the background were the shapes of the lumpy, twisted cones, pale against the dim sky.

✦

A very different sky, sunny, and blue as forget-me-nots, was visible through the window of the palace bed chamber where Jinks the acrobat lay.

But Jinks was not interested in the view. He was interested only in the delicious broth being fed to him by Sharn, and in telling the story of his heroic but vain efforts to save Lief from death.

'Of course I would never have left him, had I not seen him die. I would willingly have laid down my own life for my king!' he wailed, rolling his eyes. 'And for his friend, poor brave Barda, too, though Barda was often thoughtlessly cruel to me, rest his soul.'

His freshly-bathed hands clutched the sheet of the soft bed to which he had been carried. His eyelids fluttered as he opened his mouth to receive the spoonful of broth that Sharn was holding out to him. He swallowed, sighed and opened his mouth again.

Sharn forced back the tears that were burning behind her eyes. She tried to concentrate on Doom's last words to her, before he set off for the Os-Mine Hills with the giant woman Lindal of Broome.

'I know Jinks of old, Sharn,' Doom had said, pressing her hand. 'He will say and do anything that serves his purpose. Parts of his story are true, no doubt, but not all. Lief may be in danger, but he still lives, I am certain of it. We will find him, never fear.'

Sharn gave Jinks the last spoonful of broth, and shook her head slightly. She wished she could share Doom's certainty.

No doubt Doom believes Lief is alive because the Shadow Lord has not invaded Deltora, Sharn thought. But even the Shadow Lord is not all-knowing. His spies have told him that Lief and the Belt are safe in Tora, and he believes it. His attention is not focused on us. For now. But that could change at any time. Any time . . .

She put aside the empty bowl. When she turned back to the bed, she saw that her patient's eyes were closed, and that he was breathing slowly and evenly. Jinks had fallen asleep, it seemed.

Sharn shut her own eyes. Her head was throbbing.

She knew she should get up and go downstairs. There was so much to do. There were still crowds of people in the entrance hall. And by now Marilen would be waiting in her room for her midday meal. Her tray would have to be fetched from the kitchen. Then the poor girl would have to be told, as gently as possible, of the news Jinks had brought. Sharn dreaded the very thought of that.

I will stay here and rest, just for a little while, she said to herself.

Jinks opened his eyes a crack. He peered out from under his eyelashes and saw Sharn still sitting quietly beside him, her head bowed. He almost cursed aloud in annoyance.

What was the woman doing, just sitting there? Did she have no work to do? He had expected her to creep out of the room as soon as she thought he was asleep. Not go to sleep herself!

He considered groaning to disturb her, then decided it would be unwise to do this immediately. After all, he had just pretended to fall peacefully asleep.

Be patient, Jinks, my boy, he told himself. You do not want to make her suspicious, do you? Wake her later if you need to, but for now keep your eyes shut and your mouth closed. And while you are doing that, you can use that mighty brain of yours to make your plan perfect.

6 - Dread

E very nerve in Lief's body was telling him that all was not well in Del. Paddling in the dimming light, with Jasmine beside him, the spiders mercifully sleeping in their cages at the bottom of the boat, and Barda resting in the stern, he had tried to relax. But the feeling of dread had been growing for the past hour. It was impossible to ignore.

He had tried telling himself that it was caused by the gloom through which the little boat was moving. Where once there had been shimmering rainbows, now there was only sullen dullness.

But he knew that this was not the whole answer. The words 'Danger' and 'Del' kept stealing into his mind hand in hand, tormenting him.

'I do not like this,' muttered Barda, breaking the long silence. 'I fear the Aurons have sensed us, and have dimmed the light so as to be able to take us unawares.'

Lief made no reply.

Jasmine turned to look at him. 'You are plainly not with us, Lief,' she said coldly. 'Could you not speak of what is on your mind, for once?'

Lief sighed. 'I keep feeling there is trouble in Del,' he said, giving in to the temptation to voice his thoughts. 'I would give much to be able to tell Mother and Doom and—and others in the palace who may be worrying—where we are.'

'It is a little late to think of that,' snapped Jasmine. She knew only too well who Lief meant by 'others'. He meant the girl he was to marry. The girl he had chosen from 'one of the best Toran families', as Jinks had put it, to be his queen.

How can he think I do not know of her? she thought resentfully. *Everyone* is gossiping of the marriage plans, according to Jinks.

Then she realised, with a start, that Lief had said 'others *in the palace*'. So his bride-to-be was already in Del! Lief had brought her with him when he returned from Tora.

Then he left her almost at once, to pursue me, Jasmine thought. And he has not returned. How she must hate me for that. And Sharn and Doom must hate me, too, for delaying the marriage that was to give Deltora an heir, make it safe.

For the first time she faced the fact that her hasty rush to the Os-Mine Hills might have disastrous results for her country.

Because of me, Lief is in danger, she thought. And

that means that Deltora is in terrible danger too. I have my reasons for trying to reach the Shadowlands. The best of reasons! A little sister I never knew I had. A sister who is depending on me to save her. But I did not intend others to suffer by my actions.

Guilt pierced her heart. And the guilt made her angry.

'I did not ask you and Barda to come rushing after me, Lief!' she said harshly. 'If you had not, I would be dead, certainly. But Deltora would have been safe. And your . . . your friends . . . would have had no need to fear.'

Lief frowned. To him, Jasmine's anger seemed quite unreasonable. Why should she flare up like this, when all he had said was that he wished he could send a message home?

'Surely I have told you often enough, Jasmine, that, far from blaming you for anything, I am *grateful* to you!' he exclaimed. 'If we had not followed you we would never have found the Pirran Islands.'

Receiving no reply, he grew even more irritated. 'As soon as you told me that the Shadowlands prisoners were in danger I agreed to move on at once, did I not? Without returning to Del to get help? What more could you ask of me?'

Jasmine sniffed.

'When you two have finished sniping at one another,' growled Barda from the stern, 'you may care to look at what is ahead.'

Lief's stomach tightened as he obeyed. A large, low, spreading shape was slowly becoming visible through the dimness. It was very close. They had come upon it all unknowing.

'Land!' he breathed.

'Yes,' Barda muttered. 'And this time it may well be Auron. In this gloom we might easily have rounded a cavern wall without seeing it. We had better be prepared.'

+

At the same moment, in Del, Sharn was roused by the sound of Jinks moaning. She had no idea of how much time had passed since she began to doze, but she knew very well that the moans were intended to attract her attention.

She looked down at Jinks.

'Are you in pain?' she enquired, a little impatiently. 'Perhaps you need another dose of my herbal cure? I know the taste is not pleasant, but—'

'Oh no, my lady!' Jinks cried hastily 'The pain has quite gone, thanks to you. But I am still as weak as a baby, and my memories torment me!'

Sharn looked concerned. Jinks fluttered his eyelashes and sighed.

'Please do not feel you have to stay with me,' he whispered pathetically. 'I need only a good, long sleep. This evening I could perhaps force down a little ale, if you would bring it to me. A glass or two might settle my nerves.'

'I will leave you then,' said Sharn, rising to her feet. 'Sleep well.'

Sharn was no fool. She was certain that Jinks was pretending to be far more unwell than he was, so as to be assured of a soft bed, plentiful food and tender nursing. He had a few cuts and bruises, and his feet were blistered. That was all.

But it suited her that the acrobat should stay where he was for now. It was vital that the news he had brought to the palace did not spread and reach the Shadow Lord's ears.

The other people who had been in the kitchen when Jinks arrived would be no problem. Lindal was with Doom. Josef and Ranesh had been sworn to secrecy, then taken back to the library. They would not be permitted to venture downstairs again until Doom's return.

And Amarantz? Amarantz, completely deaf, had not heard a word Jinks had said.

I admit I am grateful for that, Sharn thought. Amarantz is a good cook and a willing worker as well as a good friend. I would be sorry to have to hide *her* away upstairs.

She put her hand to the knob of the bed chamber door. But as she did so the knob turned, the door opened, and Marilen hurried into the room.

'I heard your voice, Sharn,' Marilen began. 'I have been looking for you everywhere! I must—'

'Marilen—why are you here?' cried Sharn, trying to shield the girl from the bed. 'Please, I beg you, go back to your room. I know you must be hungry, but I will bring your tray to you as soon as I am able.'

Marilen stood her ground. 'Doom brought me my meal before he left,' she said shortly. 'I must speak with you, Sharn. It is very urgent. I—'

She broke off as she caught sight of Jinks, who had struggled to a sitting position so as to see her more clearly. 'Doom told me that a man called Jinks is claiming that Lief is dead,' she said abruptly. 'Is this he? Is this Jinks?'

'Indeed, my lady, to my great grief,' whimpered Jinks. With a tiny groan he fell back on his pillows, his hand to his brow. His eyes, alive with curiosity, gleamed as he watched Marilen between his fingers.

'You are a liar!' the girl snapped. 'Why are you playing this trick?' She was holding herself very straight. Her voice was filled with contempt. Her beautiful face was stern.

She has grown up very rapidly in the past weeks, thought Sharn, with something of a shock. How is it that I have not noticed? Oh, why did Doom have to tell her? I did not know he had seen her before he left.

'Has this man been left alone at any time since he arrived in the palace, Sharn?' Marilen demanded. 'Even for a moment?'

Sharn shook her head. 'Please leave us, Marilen,' she said in a low voice. 'I must go downstairs now, but I will come to you as soon as I can.'

Marilen hesitated, then nodded. 'Please hurry. I will

be in the library,' she said. With another contemptuous glance at Jinks, she turned and stalked from the room.

'Poor young lady,' murmured Jinks. 'My news has affected her deeply, it seems.'

'All who fear the Shadow Lord must be deeply affected, Jinks,' said Sharn, struggling to keep her voice even. She left the room, the door closing with a soft click behind her.

The moment he was alone, Jinks threw back the covers and scrambled from the bed. He padded to the door on his bandaged feet and twisted the knob.

The door was locked. He was a prisoner.

Jinks frowned. Here was something unexpected. Sharn, for all her soft words, did not trust him.

This did not suit his plans at all.

'You think you have me where you want me, my lady,' he muttered aloud. 'But you will find that Jinks is not so easily outwitted.'

Quickly he began to search the room.

7 - Truth and Lies

Far away, in the secret sea, Jasmine leaned forward, peering at the land ahead. She murmured to Kree, who spread his wings and soared into the air. The companions watched as the bird sped low towards the dark, mysterious mass.

Suddenly, something shot upwards from the water. Kree seemed to stop dead in mid-air. And the next moment the boat was rocking violently as Jasmine leaped to her feet, shrieking. For Kree was plummeting, wings fluttering helplessly, into the sea.

'Jasmine!' roared Barda. 'You will have us over!'

Lights flared in the darkness ahead. There was the sound of shouting, and splashing.

Jasmine threw herself down, seized her paddle and plunged it into the water. 'Lief, help me!' she cried. 'Make haste! Kree will drown!'

'No!' Barda roared. 'Turn the boat! Get us away!'

But Lief paid no heed to either of them. He had

dropped his paddle and was reaching for his sword. Dozens of long, pale forms were streaking through the water towards them, like enormous spears veiled with foam.

'Beware!' he shouted. And had no time to say more. For in seconds the attackers were upon them, surging from the water amid fountains of spray.

Lief gripped his sword, knowing that to use it would be fatal. The boat was surrounded by a ring of huge, sharp-fanged silver eels. Their wicked mouths gaped wide, streaming with water. And hunched on the neck of each one was a wild-eyed, dog-faced being clothed in grey animal skins. The beings' hands, tattooed from wrist to fingertip, held long, thin spears of sharpened bone, poised to strike.

A dripping black bundle was thrown carelessly into the boat. It was Kree. The bird struggled pitifully at Jasmine's feet, one wing trailing. With a cry, Jasmine bent to him. The spear arms drew back.

Lief never knew where the words came from. Pure instinct brought them to his lips. 'We are the people of Doran the Dragonlover. Do not harm us, tribe of Auron,' he gasped.

The eels stared glassily, without understanding. But the strange beings on their backs stirred. Lief was conscious of pale, slitted eyes measuring him.

'Doran sent you to us from above?' one of the Aurons asked at last.

Her voice was like a song, like water rippling over

stones. But there was warning in it.

Do not lie.

Lief swallowed, aware that at any moment a spear could plunge into his heart. 'Doran is long dead, as you must know,' he said carefully. 'His words, written in an old book, led us to you.'

'What do you seek?' asked another of the Aurons. And again the voice was full of melody, with an undercurrent of threat.

Tell the truth.

'Many of Doran's people are prisoners of the Shadow Lord,' said Lief. 'To save them, we need the Pirran Pipe.'

There was a soft, sighing sound like a wind skimming over water. The spears were lowered a little.

'The Pipe is in three parts,' said the first Auron to have spoken.

Do not lie.

Lief nodded. 'We already have one part,' he said quietly. 'We have come to beg you for the second, though we were told you would not give it.'

The Auron glanced at her friends. Then she turned back to Lief. Her tattooed hands tightened on her spear, and slowly turned its point downward.

'You were told truly,' she said. 'Come with us.'

+

As their boat was towed to shore, the companions saw, to their astonishment, that the 'island' was not an island at all. It was a mass of rafts, bound together to form one vast platform crowded with mud-brick dwellings.

The edge of the platform was thronged with people. Many held torches that smoked and flickered, giving off an oily, fishy smell. Small children, yawning and rubbing their eyes, hid behind the adults' legs. Older children stood in groups, very upright and stern, short bone spears at the ready.

Behind the crowd rose a low tower open on all sides. At the top of the tower stood two shadowy figures. One of these was wearing long robes and a tall headdress.

The Piper of Auron, Lief thought. Keeper of the stem of the Pirran Pipe. He watched as the Piper turned and spoke. He saw the companion hesitate, then finally bow. An instruction, it seemed, had been given and accepted.

'This is Auron?' Barda muttered, as they clambered out of the boat.

Lief looked about him. Everywhere there were signs that the people had been woken by the intruders. The newly lit torches. The heavy-eyed children. The doors of the dwellings hanging open, as if the inhabitants had rushed out in alarm.

'It is certainly a place where Aurons *live*,' he murmured back. 'But it cannot be Auron itself. The map makes it clear that Auron is a true island.'

'Then where are we?' Jasmine demanded. She had climbed up beside them and now stood looking around warily, Kree cradled in her arms.

'I think this platform is the dotted outline on the map,' Lief whispered. 'Doran used a broken line to show

51

that its position is not fixed. It is anchored now, but no doubt it moves around when the people wish it.'

'Why do they not live on their island?' Jasmine demanded fiercely, not troubling to lower her voice. 'Are they so savage and careless that they have made it unfit to support life?'

Lief nudged her violently, but it was too late. Many in the crowd had heard her, and were frowning and muttering among themselves.

Jasmine's eyes flashed green fire. 'I do not care what they think!' she spat. 'They struck Kree down for no reason. Who would do such a thing to a creature who meant no harm?'

'Those who did not *know* he meant no harm,' said a quiet voice beside Lief. 'Those who have never seen a bird in their lives, and who have learned, through bitter experience, that what is unknown may be deadly.'

Lief swung around. A pair of shrewd eyes met his own. Instinctively, he knew that this was one of the figures he had seen in the tower. The Piper's companion.

'My name is Penn,' the Auron said. 'I am the history-keeper of the rafts. The Piper has appointed me to be your host.'

'Our gaoler, you mean!' flashed Jasmine.

Penn smiled, showing two rows of chipped, pointed teeth. 'Whatever I am, I am all you have,' she said simply. 'It would be wise for you to follow me, now, to a safe place. The crowd's mood is growing ugly.'

✦

As Lief, Barda and Jasmine followed Penn through the narrow pathways of the rafts, Jinks ran on tiptoe through the hallways of the second floor of the palace.

The long, strong hair pin he had found at the back of a drawer had helped him escape from his own bed chamber. Now it was time to carry out his plans.

He knew he had plenty of time. Even if Sharn came upstairs again, she would not stop on the second floor. She would go straight up to the library to see what that Toran spitfire, Marilen, wanted.

There was no doubt in his mind that Marilen was Lief's bride-to-be. How exciting it had been to see the message on the slate that old fool had been holding up in the kitchen!

And now Jinks had seen the girl for himself. A pert little minx she is, too, he thought resentfully. How dare she call me a liar? As it happens, I *am* lying. But for all she knows, I am telling the honest truth!

He reached the last door in the hallway and began to work on the lock with his hairpin. Lief probably *is* dead by now, in any case, he thought. But whether he is or not, my pleasant life in the palace is over. It is very unfair, but there it is.

He closed his eyes, jiggling the lock, as his thoughts ran over familiar ground. Yes, Jinks, he told himself, you must face facts. If Lief is alive, he will return and tell everyone that you abandoned him. Then you will be finished. And if Lief is dead, the Shadow Lord will come, and the palace itself is finished.

With satisfaction, he heard the lock give way with a gentle click. He entered the room, carefully closing the door behind him.

A blue cloak hanging on a hook in one corner told him that the room was Sharn's. Good! Rapidly Jinks began to go through shelves and drawers.

I will search all the rooms and take what I fancy, he thought. By the time the losses are discovered I will be riding west on a stolen horse, my saddlebags stuffed with valuables. And in the west I will find a nice, safe hiding place where a rich acrobat who is not too choosy about his friends can enjoy a well-earned retirement.

Closing the last of the drawers, he saw with annoyance that his search had yielded only a few coins, a topaz brooch and a gold chain upon which hung a locket containing a tiny portrait of King Endon, Lief's father, as a young man.

Jinks snorted in disgust. Why, the king's mother still dressed like a blacksmith's wife! Where were the jewels, gold rings and ropes of pearls he had expected to find?

Shaking his head, he hurried out of the room and moved to the next door.

Do not fret, Jinks, my boy, he told himself, inserting his handy hairpin into the lock. The girl Marilen's room must be here somewhere.

The gossip was that Lief had chosen the finest of the royal jewels for his bride. But Marilen had not been wearing anything of value when Jinks saw her. So the jewels must be hidden away in her room. What a prize *they* would be!

The lock clicked under the pressure of his fingers, and he entered the second room.

It looked almost as bare as the first. But on a low table by the fire was a tray holding a bowl of stew, a salad, some bread, and, best of all, a small golden-brown cake in a silver paper case.

Jinks hurried to the table, reached for the cake, then drew back. A folded paper was lying beside the tray. Clearly it had not yet been read, for its wax seal was only partly broken. Eyes sharp with curiosity, Jinks opened it.

> *My dearest Marilen,*
>
> *We in Tora can no longer share your thoughts. The distance that separates us is too great. But your last letter made me uneasy, for it said nothing of your feelings, or of Lief. I fear there is something troubling you— something that you cannot, or dare not, put into words. I pray that all is well.*
>
> *I am writing to say that Zeean and I will be travelling to Del within the next few days. I know you will be delighted by this news, my dear, and will tell all those who need to know of it.*
>
> *Your loving father*

Jinks grinned in delight. So he had stumbled on Marilen's room already! He should have realised it at once, because of the tray. The spoilt wench had stormed off to find Sharn, leaving her meal untouched.

He grabbed the cake and gobbled it down with relish.

Now, to find the jewels! He looked around, enjoying the moment. Then, with shock and disbelief, he felt a stab of pain, agonising pain, in his stomach. Gasping, he doubled up, clutching his belly as the pain stabbed again, and again. He tried to call out, but could manage only a croaking whisper.

Agony gripped him. He fell writhing to the floor, his fingers clawing on the thin rug, his heels kicking at the table.

The table tilted. The tray slid over the edge.

By the time it hit the ground, Jinks was dead.

8 - The House of Penn

Thoughts of Del had again begun nagging at Lief as he followed Penn through the maze of narrow walkways that ran between the crowded dwellings of the rafts. But they were driven from his mind the moment he, Jasmine and Barda entered the history-keeper's hut.

The hut was small but pleasant, despite the strong smell of fish oil that drifted both from the stove burning in one corner and the shell lamp fixed to a wall.

A sleeping hammock covered with a patchwork rug of grey skins hung from hooks fastened to the low ceiling. There was no other furniture at all, but the floor was covered with a beautiful mat woven in soft sea colours.

Three of the smooth, pale walls were covered with hanging baskets in which rolled parchments, clothes and other belongings were neatly arranged. The door wall was bare except for a hook upon which Penn invited

Lief to hang his cloak, a curtained window and a small wall hanging woven in a strange, bold pattern.

Below the wall hanging was a large blue bowl filled with water. Inside the bowl, two small, upright sea creatures swayed amid fronds of silver weed. They were very like sea horses in shape, but glittered with every colour of the rainbow.

'My companions, Tresk and Mesk,' said Penn, leaning over the bowl. Plainly, by the way she cooed and smiled at the little creatures as they bobbed up to nuzzle her hand, bubbling eagerly, they were very dear to her.

She looked anxious as Filli crept out from under Jasmine's collar and ran down to the edge of the bowl to investigate.

'Filli would not harm them,' Jasmine assured her. But Penn did not relax until Filli was safely back on Jasmine's shoulder again, nibbling at a dried berry from Jasmine's pocket.

After that, Penn busied herself in making her guests welcome. She could not have been more helpful, or more agreeable.

She took down the hammock and stored it away, to make more room. Then she supplied Jasmine with everything necessary to care for Kree's injured wing. All the while she asked questions about Deltora and the companions' present journey, listening alertly to their answers.

Finally, once Kree was resting comfortably, she

brought large snail shells of strong, oily soup to her guests.

'It is not to your taste, perhaps?' she asked anxiously, as she watched them drink.

'Oh, no, it is very good,' Lief assured her, trying not to wrinkle his nose. He felt something hard on his tongue and removed it. It was a shrivelled claw. He stared at it with repulsion, wondering what horrible creature it had come from.

Penn looked grave. 'You would be wise always to speak the truth on the rafts,' she said gently. 'As a keeper of history, who has read much of what Doran taught our ancestors, I am familiar with your people's ways. But in this I am different from most. Even politeness, which in the world above, I believe, is thought good, is no excuse for lies here.'

She gestured to the wall-hanging which had fascinated Lief ever since he entered the hut.

Lief, Barda and Jasmine stared at the bold symbols, and at last saw the word concealed within them.

'Truth,' Lief murmured.

Penn nodded. 'Beauty is important to us, as befits followers of the Piper Auron,' she said. 'But we believe that nothing can be truly beautiful unless truth dwells within it. Lies and pretence have been the ruin of our people in the past. Now our children are taught from their earliest days that truth is all-important, and lying is the greatest sin.'

She smiled slightly. 'So, tell me. Are you really enjoying the meal you have been given?'

'Well, if you want the truth, while I am grateful for your kindness, I find it repulsive!' growled Barda, putting down his shell.

'And I,' said Jasmine, doing likewise.

Lief sighed. 'Truly the most unpleasant brew I have ever tasted,' he agreed.

Penn's smile broadened. 'It is written that Doran felt the same at first,' she chuckled. Quickly she drained her own shell, crunching the dregs with relish.

'And now,' she said, with obvious reluctance, putting the shell aside, 'it is my task to tell you why we cannot help you.'

Lief leaned forward. 'Could we not speak to your Piper? Our cause is just, and we would have your part of the Pirran Pipe for only—'

Penn raised her arm, which was covered in complicated tattoos almost to the elbow.

'Do not waste your breath in argument,' she said bluntly. 'The Piper knows why you are here. The guards who were not needed for towing your boat landed long before you, and informed him.'

She sighed at the expression on Lief's face.

'The Piper wishes you to know that we would give you anything you asked, if we could. Your kinsman

Doran spent much time on the rafts in ages past. He gave our ancestors many gifts, including the gift of fire, without which our lives today would be miserable beyond words.'

Barda frowned. 'Then—'

Penn shrugged. 'Do you think that we would live like this if our part of the Pirran Pipe was with us?' she sighed. 'Do you think we *choose* to drift the seas, spending half our lives searching for materials to mend the rafts? Do you think we *choose* to live in darkness, when our souls long for light?'

Lief struggled with warring feelings of disbelief and bitter disappointment. He knew the second part of the Pipe was near. He could feel it! Yet he knew also that Penn, whose people valued truth above all things, could not be lying.

'The stem of the Pipe is lost, then?' he asked, in a level voice.

'Lost to us,' said Penn. 'It is on the island of Auron. And that is lost to us, also.'

'*Lost?*' Jasmine shook her head impatiently. '*How* lost? Has it sunk into the sea? Has it been overrun by the monsters you bred to—'

'Monsters *we* bred?' cried Penn. Pale eyes flashing, all stiffness forgotten, she jumped to her feet. 'Who has told you this lie?' she thundered, looking down at Jasmine angrily.

Then her face changed. Her eyes narrowed, and her wide mouth hardened. 'Ah, of course,' she hissed. 'Those accursed Plumes, who could not speak the truth if their lives depended upon it. Who would stop at nothing to smear our name to descendants of Doran!'

'If the Plumes were lying, they did not know it,' snapped Jasmine, refusing to be cowed. 'They told us only what they truly believed.'

Penn glared at her for a moment. Then, slowly, her rage seemed to die, and her face relaxed. 'I am sorry for my anger,' she said, walking to the window, pulling aside the curtain and staring out at the dimness. 'I was wrong to blame you. The Plumes are clever deceivers.'

Jasmine looked as if she was going to argue further, but Lief spoke quickly, before she had the chance. Hope was again flaring in his heart. For if the second part of the Pirran Pipe was on Auron, it could surely be won, whatever the danger that guarded it.

'Tell us, Penn, I beg you, why you say Auron is lost,' he urged.

Strange, high, echoing calls began to drift through the window, filling the room, growing louder every moment.

Penn turned around. Her face was shadowed with weariness and something more. Despair, perhaps.

'Dawn is being sung by the Piper,' she said. 'The time of sleep is over. Not that any of us have *had* our proper sleep, this night.'

'I am sorry—' Lief began, but Penn waved away his apology and walked to the hanging baskets on the back wall. She selected two small, ragged pieces of parchment, then moved to the door.

'Come,' she said. 'Your boat may now leave the rafts with safety.'

'We cannot leave!' exclaimed Jasmine, glancing protectively at Kree. 'Kree must rest further. He is still weak.'

'The bird may remain where he is,' said Penn, her serious face relaxing a little as she regarded Jasmine's earnest face. 'In his condition he will not trouble Tresk and Mesk, and you will be back before the Piper calls down the night. To swim would be faster, but not for you, I suspect. I am taking you to Auron.'

Lief's heart jolted with excitement. He glanced at Barda, whose face was bright with triumph.

Penn's shrewd eyes seemed to dim as she watched them. 'I do not look forward to the journey,' she murmured. 'I had hoped to avoid it. But you must see the island for yourselves. Only then will you understand the truth.'

9 - Troubles

Not another word would Penn say. In silence she led the companions through the walkways. Curtains twitched aside as they passed, and faces filled with curiosity, fear or resentment peered out.

The back of Lief's neck burned. 'We are not welcome here,' he muttered.

'Why should you be?' said Penn calmly. 'You invaded our waters in a Plume boat, carrying the Plume part of the Pirran Pipe, to mock us. You brought fearsome creatures with you. You accused us of making Auron unfit for life. And you are very large and ugly, and smell unpleasant.'

'An attractive list of qualities,' said Barda dryly. 'I wonder you could bear to have us in your home, Penn.'

Penn shrugged. 'As I told you, I have read of your people. That was why the Piper chose me for this task.'

They reached the edge of the platform where their boat still rocked gently, tied up with a few others. Stony-faced guards moved aside, at a word from Penn, to let them pass.

The water was alive with huge, ferocious-looking eels like the ones the guards had been riding. They were cruising just below the surface, twisting together lazily.

Trying not to look at them, Lief, Jasmine and Barda climbed into the boat, taking great care not to slip. Penn followed, quite untroubled. Then she caught sight of Fury and Flash, still asleep in their cages on the floor of the boat.

'I had forgotten them, when I suggested we take your boat,' she murmured nervously. 'Their cages are strong, I suppose?'

'Very strong,' Lief assured her, taking up his paddle.

Penn shuddered and untied the boat, turning her head as she did so to stare at the eels, which she plainly found quite restful to look upon.

She pointed west. 'That way,' she said in a low voice. 'Keep a straight course. And please paddle gently. I do not distrust your word, but I would prefer that your beasts did not wake.'

The boat moved away from the platform. Ahead was dim, open sea. And Auron.

✦

A world away, in Del, the sun was sliding slowly down towards the horizon.

Sharn had been in the entrance hall for far longer than she had intended. Many, many people were waiting to speak to her.

One of these was Barda's deputy, a Resistance fighter called Mobley, who wished to report a death. Pieter, the brother of one of the helpers in the entrance hall, had died horribly when two Plains scorpions escaped from a box he had hidden under his shirt.

'We think it was Pieter who put the scorpion in the king's bed chamber, ma'am,' Mobley said. 'In the old days he was a roof-mender. He could have easily climbed to the king's window and cut the bars. Also, we found this in the scorpions' box. Maria says it is her brother's writing.'

He showed a scrap of paper.

the king must die the King must die the King must die the King must die the King must die the King must die the King must die the King must die the King must die the King must die the King

'But why would Maria's brother feel this way?' Sharn exclaimed, amazed and distressed.

Mobley shrugged. 'Who knows? Like many other folk, he and Maria lost each other the night the Shadow Lord took over the city. They only met again by chance, when Pieter wandered into the palace a few weeks ago. He was thin as a rail, had no memory, and suffered from headaches, bad headaches that gave him no peace.'

He paused. 'It was a terrible thing Pieter did, ma'am, but as I saw him lying there it came into my mind that if things had been different, I could have gone the same way as he did. I, too, lost my family in the troubles. It was only joining up with the Resistance that kept me sane, I think.'

Sharn hurried upstairs at last, and went directly to the library. There she found Marilen sitting at one of the tables. Josef, looking harried and distressed, was checking books nearby, with Ranesh silently assisting him.

When Marilen saw Sharn, she stood up at once. Her face was very pale. 'We will talk in my bed chamber, if you please,' she said formally.

They moved down the great staircase in strained silence. As they reached the second floor, and the guards who barred the stairs stepped aside to let them pass, Marilen swallowed and seemed to make a great effort to calm herself.

'Forgive me, Sharn, if I seem to be behaving oddly,' she whispered. 'I went to the library for comfort while I waited for you. But I must speak to you in privacy. Josef and Ranesh—especially Ranesh—must not hear what I have to say. And I believe it is dangerous to speak aloud out here.'

She hastened towards the hallway which led to her own room. Sharn followed, greatly troubled. What had made Marilen think the hallways were not safe? This floor had been searched very thoroughly for listening devices.

But even stranger was Marilen's determination not to speak where Josef and Ranesh might hear. Sharn had assumed that the girl wanted only to discuss the report of Lief's death. But Josef and Ranesh knew about that already.

What else could she have to tell me? Sharn thought. And why does she say that Ranesh, in particular, should not know of it?

Marilen had reached her door and drawn out her key. But when she put the key in the lock, she drew back.

'It is already unlocked,' she whispered.

Before Sharn could stop her, she had twisted the knob and thrown the door wide. There was a moment's horrified silence. Then Marilen gave a single, piercing cry and buried her face in her hands. Sharn simply stared, shocked and silent.

Jinks lay sprawled amid a small wreckage of broken china and spoiled food. His eyes stared sightlessly at the ceiling. His mouth was twisted in a snarl of agony. From the pocket of his trousers spilled part of a fine gold chain with a locket hanging from it.

Sharn looked down at it. 'My locket,' she said slowly, trying to make sense of what she was seeing. Then, pulling herself together, she moved past Marilen and knelt by Jinks, feeling for his pulse.

After a moment she stood up. 'He is dead,' she said evenly. 'He must have been more badly injured than we, or he himself, thought. His heart—'

'No,' said Marilen. 'Poison.' She stooped to pick up a crumpled silver paper case from the floor. She held it out to Sharn, her face very pale.

'Poison!' Sharn gaped at her.

'That was what I was going to tell you, Sharn,' said Marilen, the words at last tumbling out. 'As soon as I uncovered the tray, I knew I must not eat the food.'

'But—but—' Sharn ran a trembling hand over her brow. So many questions were rushing through her mind. She managed to blurt out one. 'Marilen, how could you know?'

Marilen shrank back, wrapping her arms around her body, as though to protect herself from attack. Then she seemed to find the strength to answer. She unfolded her arms and lifted her chin. 'I am a daughter of Tora,' she said.

'I too am a daughter of Tora,' said Sharn, staring at her. 'Or, at least, my ancestors were Toran, so I was always told. But can Toran magic sense poison?'

'All I can tell you is that I knew at once that there was poison in the meal, and I did not eat it,' replied Marilen quietly.

She gestured at the rigid body on the floor. 'The man Jinks came here to steal. He stole once too often, and it was his death. But *I* was the intended victim.'

Sharn forced her face into a calm she did not feel. Her mind was racing. 'Do you wish to leave here, Marilen?' she asked at last. 'Do you wish to return to Tora?'

She waited tensely for the answer.

But Marilen shook her head. 'No,' she said firmly. 'That would be to give in to our enemies. Whoever tried to kill me may not know exactly who I am, but at least

69

wishes to make trouble between Deltora's east and west. And who could that be, but a servant of the Shadow Lord?'

'You are right,' murmured Sharn, impressed and moved by the girl's courage.

'So there is a spy in our midst,' said Marilen. 'A spy who has somehow discovered that I am here.'

She glanced at the body on the floor. 'I thought it was Jinks, but plainly that is not so,' she added coolly.

Sharn swallowed. She felt almost timid, facing this girl who seemed to have changed into a strong woman in a matter of days.

'You suspect—Ranesh?' she asked quietly.

Marilen coloured to the roots of her hair. It was as though, in a moment, she had become a young girl again.

'Oh, no!' she gasped. 'How can you say such a thing? Ranesh would never seek to harm me. On the contrary, if he was to find out my life had been threatened, he would ... he would do something foolish, I am sure of it. So he must not know.'

She turned quickly away, pretending to straighten the tie at her waist.

Ah, thought Sharn. So that is how things stand. Well, this complicates things even further.

A wave of immense weariness washed over her.

Lief, where are you? she thought. Oh, where are you?

10 - The Dome

Lief was paddling towards the island of Auron, his mind filled with music. His shoulders were aching, but he was no longer aware of it. He could only think of the sound, which was growing stronger every moment.

'Lief, what is the matter?' asked Jasmine. Lief glanced at her. Her familiar face wavered in front of his glazed eyes like a face in a dream.

'He feels the magic of the Pirran Pipe,' Penn said from the front of the boat. She leaned forward and tapped Lief sharply on the knee. 'Lief! Wake!' she commanded.

The tap, and the piercing voice, went some way towards cutting through the dreamy haze that clouded Lief's mind. He blinked and murmured. Penn put her hand over the side, scooped up some water and threw it at him.

Lief gasped as the cold drops spattered over his face.

Suddenly he was fully conscious again. Conscious, but confused and furiously angry.

'Why did you do that?' he shouted, glaring at Penn and roughly shaking off Jasmine's restraining hand.

'It was necessary,' said Penn calmly. 'I have not brought you all this way to have you miss your first sight of Auron.'

Breathing hard, Lief wiped the water from his eyes. Slowly his wild anger died. He realised where he was, and what had happened.

'I am sorry,' he mumbled, filled with shame.

'The fault is mine,' said Penn, still in that same calm voice. 'I should have warned you, but I was taken by surprise. The Pipe's spell is more powerful than I have ever felt it, no doubt because of the mouthpiece you carry. I have been struggling with it myself.'

Only then did Lief see that her own face was wet, and that her small, tattooed hands were bleeding where she had driven her sharp nails into the palms.

'There is something ahead,' Jasmine exclaimed, pointing into the gloom.

For a few moments there was silence. Then Lief and Barda cried out at the same moment as they saw what Jasmine had seen. A faint glow showed through the dimness.

'That is Auron,' said Penn, her voice trembling a little. 'Go gently, now. We must not cross the line.'

'The line?' cried Lief. 'But can we not land? Penn, we *must* land. We must see . . .'

'You will see enough, do not fear,' Penn muttered.

The boat crawled forward. A strange, unpleasant odour began to creep into the companions' nostrils—a thick smell of decay that seemed to stick to their clothes, to sink into their skin and cling to their hair.

Then they began to hear the gentle sound of lapping water. Other sounds, too. Soft, squelching sounds, and a sort of clicking, like the creaking of stiff joints.

The glow grew a little brighter. It spread until it was almost filling their view. Lief squinted at it, trying to see through it to the island. He saw nothing but a vast, high dome of dim light. And, to the left of the light, just where he would have expected to see it, a rugged cavern wall jutting out into the sea.

'There is the line,' breathed Penn. 'Stop!'

The companions tore their eyes from the light and looked down at the water ahead.

A broad band of bright pink and yellow seaweed floated directly in front of the boat. The band stretched away to left and right, curving to encircle the glowing dome and the odd, milky sea that surrounded it.

'You plant this weed as a warning?' exclaimed Barda. 'Ah, if only we had known this before!'

But Penn was intent on Jasmine and Lief. 'Turn the boat so its side faces the island,' she ordered. 'And, for your life, do not let it drift into the warning zone.'

So urgent was her tone that Lief did not even think of disobeying her. And the glaring pink and yellow of the weed, clearly visible even in the gloom, brought back memories that were their own warning.

'Now, look,' Penn said quietly. 'Look carefully, and understand.'

Lief stared. And as his eyes grew accustomed to the light, as they searched vainly for the shapes of rocks, hills, or anything he could recognise, his spine began to tingle.

There was nothing to be seen beneath the dome. The dome was a barrier of shimmering energy that hid everything beneath it.

Oily, shallow water, lightly steaming, lapped the dome's base, where pitted lumps of some thick substance moved sluggishly in the tide and unseen things squelched and chewed. Everything seemed covered by a milky haze, like mould. The foul smell rolled over Lief in waves.

He heard Barda curse softly, and Jasmine murmur in disbelief. Despair settled over him like a dull grey cloud.

He twisted in his seat to look at Penn. She was staring fixedly at her hands folded in her lap.

'The dome is sealed by magic,' she muttered. 'It cannot be penetrated.'

She raised her head. 'Do you understand?' she said softly. 'We of the rafts are exiles. Our ancestors were expelled from the dome long, long ago.'

'Why?' Barda asked bluntly.

Penn hunched her narrow shoulders. 'They were dangerous. They were sick of pretence,' she muttered, speaking haltingly as if every word was being forced from her. 'They wished—to make a life outside, in a place that was not what they were used to, but which had its own savage beauty.'

Lief, Barda and Jasmine looked around uncertainly. It was difficult to understand how anyone could find beauty in this overwhelming gloom.

Penn looked around also, her eyes glazed with sorrow. 'When first the rafts were made, the cavern walls shone like stars of a thousand different colours,' she whispered. 'The eels danced in a glittering rainbow sea. The writings say that it was beautiful beyond words.'

She sighed deeply. 'Even when I was a child, it was still a shadow of what it had been. I well remember the colours. But now, they are gone.'

Lief, Barda and Jasmine thought of the exquisite opal beauty through which they had sailed when first they left the territory of the Plumes. The dazzling colours that had faded as the Plumes' light failed.

Then, they had thought that the Aurons had dimmed their own light for some evil purpose. Now they knew differently.

'What happened?' Jasmine asked.

Slowly, almost unwillingly, Penn took out the two scraps of parchment she had brought from the hut. She handed them to Lief, with the lantern.

'Part of the story is here,' she muttered. 'I wrote it, in simple form, for the children of the rafts. I brought these because—because I knew you would have questions, and it would give me pain to answer them.'

Again she looked down at her hands. Her body was rigid, and her mouth was pressed into a hard line.

Lief and Jasmine looked at the first piece of parchment. Barda crept forward to look over their shoulders.

How the Rafts Came To Be

When the three Pirran tribes fled their ancient land after the coming of the Shadow Lord, they found refuge on islands in an underground sea. The Isle of Auron was well separated from the enemy islands of Plume and Keras. It was large, had natural water, and was covered by fast-growing fungus trees from which boats and dwellings could be made. When lit by the magic of the people, the cavern in which it lay shone with every colour of the rainbow.

Some Aurons found a strange, wild beauty in the island and the shining caverns. But most saw only ugliness, and at once began creating illusions of the lost beauties of Pirra. After a time, they went further. They wove a great spell, creating a dome which covered the island, containing the magic and making the illusion complete.

But there were those who did not agree with what had been done. These Aurons, our ancestors, wanted to live in a world that was real, however strange, rather than to exist in a dream created by their own minds.

Lief put down the first piece of parchment, and took up the second.

And so our ancestors were stripped of their magic and cast out as traitors. Eeran, the Piper of those days, swore that if they went in peace, so blood would not be spilled inside the dome, the caverns would always be filled with light. And our ancestors believed him, and left without a murmur.

They made rafts of driftwood lashed together with ropes of dried weed. They built mud houses, learned to live the life of the shining sea which was their home and were happy.

For many years, Eeran's promise was kept. But then, not long after the coming of Doran, the bringer of fire, the light began, very slowly, to dim. Now, centuries later, our realm is as you see it.

The dome-dwellers continue to expel all things that threaten their idea of beauty, including their dead. Thus they feed the creatures which breed around the dome. And those creatures are hunted by the Arach, those monsters of nightmare which once hid deep in caves, away from the light, but now nest in the warmth and dimness of the dome sea.

The dome is protected by the magic of the Aurons within it, and the stem of the Pirran Pipe. We, who are without magic, cannot penetrate it. Many have tried and died in the attempt.

We must all prepare for a time when the light is gone altogether. We must learn to find our way in dark water, and to know by touch the warning lines which must never be crossed. We must continue to save every scrap of wood, to mend the rafts cleverly, and to hate waste.

Then we will survive.

Lief looked up to meet Penn's grave eyes. He handed back the parchments, saying nothing. What was there to say?

But Jasmine's eyes had narrowed. 'What are these Arach?' she asked abruptly.

At the sound of the name, Penn stiffened and glanced from side to side. With a stifled cry she half rose from her seat, then fell back.

'What have I done?' she gasped. 'Oh, Auron forgive me! In my distress I forgot to watch. We are drifting over the line!'

The companions looked down. Pink and yellow weed was all around them. It was lush and thickly branched, floating just under the surface of the water. Before they could gather their wits, the boat's prow had nudged out of the weed, and into the milky water beyond.

And by the dome, something stirred. There were sounds. Sucking, creaking sounds that chilled the blood.

'Back!' muttered Penn, her eyes wild with panic. 'Make haste! Oh, make haste!'

Lief and Jasmine began back-paddling frantically. Their paddles splashed uselessly, snagging on the ragged blanket of weed. The boat swayed awkwardly from side to side, but did not move.

Without another word, Penn threw herself into the water and began clawing at the weed, flinging great trails of it aside, trying vainly to clear a path.

Two huge shadows, two vast, lumpy bodies each

swaying on eight thin, jointed legs, rose dark against the glow of the dome. Red eyes gleamed as the beasts sprang forward and began running towards the boat, running with terrifying speed over the surface of the water.

'Over the side!' Penn shouted. 'Swim! Swim for your lives!'

11 - Arach

Without hesitation, Lief caught Jasmine in his arms and tumbled with her into the weed-filled water.

Surfacing, he heard Barda splashing and shouting somewhere behind him. He shouted back, then, holding Jasmine tightly against his chest, he struck out, kicking aside the sodden cloak that clung around his legs, fighting his way through the weed.

Jasmine was gasping, choking, trying to speak.

'I know what you want to say, and you can save your breath,' Lief panted. 'I will not leave you.'

Barda came up beside him. Supporting Jasmine between them they clawed through the matted growth, struggling forward with painful slowness.

'What are you doing? Make haste!' screamed Penn from the dimness beyond the weed. Then, amazingly, she was leaving safety, plunging towards them, cutting through the water and weed like a fish.

Her head bobbed up in front of them, pale eyes wide with terror. She reached for Jasmine.

'Where is she injured?' she demanded.

'Not injured. Cannot swim!' Lief panted, and saw the history-keeper's jaw drop in stunned amazement.

Then she was swimming away, pulling Jasmine expertly along with her. And Lief and Barda were thrashing behind, hearts pounding, chests aching, through the weed and, at last, out into the open sea.

There Penn stopped and turned, treading water, supporting Jasmine easily with one arm.

'Why have you stopped?' gasped Barda.

'We are safe here,' said Penn. 'Arach do not hunt beyond the weed. The dome waters are their territory.' Then her face twisted with pain. 'Ah, no!' she wailed. 'Ah, what wicked waste!'

There was a sound like crackling dry leaves. Panting, the breath rasping in his lungs, Lief turned himself around in the water.

The Arach had halted at the edge of the seaweed band. One of them had seized the boat. It was lifting it high into the air, crushing it like paper. The other was fighting for a share, tugging at the frail craft, scrabbling inside it, looking for prey.

Lief stared, dumbfounded. The Arach were like vast, deformed spiders. Their bloated bodies were covered by glossy black shell, as though plated with armour. Their long, thin legs looked like wires of steel, prickling with spurs and spikes. Their armoured heads seemed nothing but greedy red eyes and dripping fangs.

With a dull, angry roar, the second Arach jerked violently, tearing the boat in half. Provisions, buckets, the lantern, and two small objects that Lief realised were the cages of the fighting spiders, sailed high into the air, scattering and falling with dull splashes.

Fury's cage plunged into the water just in front of Lief. Fury was scrabbling desperately inside. Lief grabbed for the cage and lifted it up, gasping as he worked at keeping himself afloat with one hand.

This is madness! he thought. I cannot save myself, let alone this spider. But he could not bring himself to let the creature drown before his eyes.

Neither, it seemed, could Barda leave Flash to his fate. Barda was floundering towards the other cage, reaching out for it as though his life depended upon it.

'The Arach have had enough,' muttered Penn.

Lief looked up and saw the monsters creeping back to the dome. The shredded remains of the boat lay scattered on the weed bed.

Without warning, Penn plunged her head under the water. Jasmine, still clasped firmly in her arm, spluttered in panic. Bubbles rose in a great stream around Penn's head and Lief thought he could hear a strange, muffled cry.

'What is she doing?' shrieked Jasmine. But Penn was already lifting her head, shaking it to clear her eyes.

In moments there was a swirling movement in the water around them. Then Lief, Barda and Jasmine were shouting in shock as four giant eels surged up from the depths, wicked mouths gaping horribly.

'Take hold of their necks,' said Penn. 'They have come in answer to my call. They will carry us home.'

✦

In a shorter time than Lief would have believed possible, they were back at the rafts. Never had he felt such speed. Never would he forget that journey—the spray beating against his face, the desperate clinging to the slippery neck of the eel.

To his shame, he had to be hauled off the eel's neck and onto the platform by the guards. He could do nothing to help himself. His legs and arms would not move. His head was spinning. The children who ducked and played like fish in the water at the platform's edge stared and giggled. The workers mending nets and weaving rope nearby sniffed in amused contempt.

Barda was in the same state as Lief himself, and Jasmine little better. Together, bedraggled, unsteady on their feet and sick at heart, they shuffled after Penn to her hut, trying to ignore the sharp-faced, silent crowd which had gathered to watch them.

The hut door was standing open. Inside, a bent figure in long robes and a tall silver head-covering stood waiting. So old, wrinkled and toothless was the face below the head-covering that if Penn had not already spoken of the Piper as 'he', Lief would not have known if he was facing a male or a female.

Penn ushered the dripping companions into the

hut, and closed the door behind them. 'Do not mind the water,' she murmured. 'This floor has been drenched more times than you could count.'

Jasmine darted at once to where Kree sat by the stove. She knelt down and lifted poor, shivering Filli from her shoulder to share the warmth. Lief and Barda took the cages containing the motionless spiders over to her, then returned to Penn's side, trying to stiffen their trembling legs.

'Well?' asked the Piper. And even in his exhaustion Lief thrilled with wonder at the sound of the voice— smooth, rich and sweet as wild honey.

Penn folded her hands, then spoke flatly, as if delivering a report. 'Tall and brave they may be, with weapons of steel,' she said. 'But in the water the males, Lief and Barda, are helpless as new-born babes, and the female, Jasmine, cannot swim at all. They would have no hope of taking the Arach by surprise, or evading them.'

She turned away. 'I have done all you require of me, Piper, and it has cost me dearly,' she muttered. 'But you must abandon your hopes.'

The Piper closed his eyes as though in pain. 'Did you tell them of my belief, Penn?' he asked softly.

Lief and Barda glanced at one another, then at Penn. What was this?

Penn was hesitating. 'No,' she said at last. 'Once I saw that they could not swim, I felt there was no need to torment them further.'

'Tell them now,' said the Piper. It was not a request, but a command.

Penn moved restlessly. 'The Piper believes that if you could reach the dome, the mouthpiece of the Pirran Pipe would give you entrance,' she said, without looking at Lief and Barda. 'He believes that the stem of the Pipe within would call to it and draw it through the magic screen. The Piper hoped—'

'I hoped many things.' The Piper opened his eyes and fixed Penn with a steely stare. 'It seems my hopes were in vain.'

But Lief had clutched Barda's arm. And Jasmine had jumped up from the floor and hurried over to them, her face alight with hope.

'Why did you not tell us this before, Penn?' she demanded. 'If we can penetrate the dome we can—'

'You cannot *reach* the dome!' cried Penn. 'You saw the Arachs! And there are many more! Their webs net the waters of their territory. The moment you enter it, the moment you touch a web, they will sense you.'

'There must be a way,' growled Barda. 'There is always—'

'There is *no* way!' shouted Penn, eyes blazing. 'In a boat, should we be so mad as to give you one, you would last only a few moments. To have any hope at all of reaching the dome you would have to swim to it underwater, beneath the webs. And you are not capable of that! Nothing is more certain.'

'The eels!' Jasmine exclaimed. 'They could surely

tow us beneath the webs. We could hold our breath for that time. They swim so fast . . .'

Penn sighed. The Piper smiled thinly. 'It could be done,' he admitted. 'If the eels could be persuaded to enter Arach territory. But they cannot. It has been tried many, many times. They will not do it.'

He shook his head in disgust. 'We knew that you would not be able to swim as we can,' he muttered. 'It is written that Doran could not defeat even our youngest children in a race. But never did we consider such weakness as this!'

He glanced back at Jasmine. 'And one of you cannot swim at all! It is—beyond belief!'

'I grew up in a forest where the only water was a shallow stream,' snapped Jasmine, heartily sick of being criticised for something she could not help. 'How could I learn to swim? Any more than you could learn to climb a tree, Piper! Or Penn could learn to swing on a vine!'

Lief gave a sharp exclamation. Jasmine swung round to him, scowling. 'I do not care what you say, Lief!' she raged. 'Palace manners might do for you, but they will not do for me. I will not be polite to these people any longer!'

But Lief's face was alight with excitement. 'Jasmine, you have it!' he exclaimed. 'Do you not see? You have told us exactly what we must do!'

12 - Suspicion

It did not take long for Lief to explain the plan that had suddenly come to him. 'You see?' he finished triumphantly. 'We do not use our weaknesses, but our strengths!'

'It is—incredible!' the Piper exclaimed, his cold eyes shining. 'It would never have crossed my mind that such a thing could be done.'

'I am not surprised. A more hare-brained idea I have never heard!' snorted Barda.

'We can do it!' Lief urged.

'We can try. And it is worth the chance,' said Jasmine. 'Unless, of course,' she added dryly, 'the Piper is wrong, and the mouthpiece of the Pirran Pipe will not allow us to penetrate the dome.'

Penn buried her face in her hands. The Piper gripped her arm. 'You must not weaken now, Penn,' Lief heard him muttering. 'They can do what we cannot. They could be our salvation!'

He turned to Lief, his hard, ancient face wearing a mild expression that Lief could not quite believe in.

'We will give you what help we can,' he said. 'If you gain the stem of the Pirran Pipe, it will be yours to keep for as long as you need it. All we ask in return is that you use your best efforts to convince the dome-dwellers to return the light to the caverns.'

It will be yours to keep for as long as you need it . . .

Those words were carefully chosen, Piper, Lief thought, studying the cold face. You speak the truth, I am sure. But for how long will we *need* the stem of the Pipe, once it is actually out of the dome? Once it is where you can lay your hands on it? No-one needs anything after they are dead. Is that your plan?

He moved his gaze to Penn's bent head. The Piper told Penn to make friends with us, he thought. So that we would want to help her people as well as ourselves. And of course she succeeded. In spite of herself.

Penn had carried out her orders reluctantly. That had been plain from the start. Perhaps she did not believe that the dome could be penetrated by the mouthpiece of the Pipe, and feared encouraging the visitors to go to their deaths.

Or perhaps Penn knew very well that once they had gained the Pipe, they would be betrayed.

'Please do not blame yourself for our decision, Penn,' he said aloud. 'We are doing only what we must.'

Penn did not raise her head.

'You accept my terms, then?' the Piper asked.

Lief met his eyes squarely. 'We will do all we can to help you once we are inside the dome, Piper. We cannot promise success. But I swear that we will beg the dome-dwellers to return your light as earnestly as we beg them for the stem of the Pirran Pipe.'

The Piper bent his head. 'I ask no more of you than that,' he murmured. He remained utterly still for a few moments, as though in the grip of strong feeling. Then he looked up, his face calm again

'You must dry yourselves, and rest,' he said. 'I will have a boat prepared. Penn? A moment, if you please.'

Penn scurried after him as he swept to the door. They went outside, and Lief saw them speaking in low voices.

'That Piper makes me uneasy,' said Barda, walking to the stove to warm his chilled hands 'He reminds me of people I knew in the Palace, in the old days. He is a schemer, and he is bending Penn to his will.'

'I think he is using us to gain the stem of the Pipe for himself,' Lief said. 'The raft-dwellers' magic, the magic that should be the birthright of every Pirran, is trapped inside the dome. But the stem of the Pipe has its own power—power which would light the caverns and do much more.'

Barda nodded agreement. 'It must seem to the Piper that fate has brought us to him, as once it brought Doran when he was needed most.'

'I agree, but—' Jasmine's brow was creased in thought. 'But why bother to deceive us, when surely there is a simpler way to gain magic? Why not seize the part of the Pipe we already have?'

Lief's hand rose, almost without his willing it, to touch the piece of knobbly wood beneath his shirt.

'I suspect that the Plume part of the Pirran Pipe is of no use to Aurons,' he said. 'They have shown no interest in it, and its power does not seem to affect them. Yet as we approached the dome, and the Auron part of the Pipe was near, Penn was clearly as moved as I was.'

Wearily he pulled off his sodden cloak, and sank down beside Kree. 'We must pretend to trust them for now, in any case,' he murmured. 'We need their help. Our first task must be to gain the stem of the Pipe. After that, we will deal with what comes.'

Penn hurried back into the room loaded with bundles and baskets. Her face was tense, her lips were strained into a smile that had no meaning.

'Here are rugs to keep you warm while you rest,' she chattered. 'And bread—freshly baked—with hot Molisk patties. I am sure you are hungry.'

She put down a basket of flat speckled rolls and a bowl of steaming objects that looked like green meatballs. Suddenly aware that they were ravenous, the companions helped themselves.

They ate with relish. The bread tasted of the sea, but was crisp and warm. The patties were delicately flavoured, and melted on the tongue.

'This meal pleases you more than the soup?' Penn asked.

'Much more,' Barda agreed, with his mouth full.

Penn's smile became a little more real. 'It is written that Doran enjoyed Molisk patties also,' she said. 'They are our festival dish. The Piper ordered them to be prepared in honour of your visit. I am glad you are having them now. Before . . .'

Her voice trailed off, and she turned away.

Lief, Barda and Jasmine looked at one another, the delicious food suddenly dry in their mouths. It was quite plain that Penn thought that the Molisk patties would be their last meal.

✦

Meanwhile, in Del, Sharn and Marilen looked down at the small body lying in the bed. Carrying Jinks back to his own chamber had been a grim task, but they had agreed that it was necessary.

'Only *we* know he was not as ill as he claimed,' Sharn said, covering the terrible face with the sheet. 'People will think that he died of his injuries.'

'The poisoner may guess the truth,' Marilen said soberly. 'And now we must try to think who that person may be. A person who knows I am here, and somehow knows who I am. And who had the opportunity to poison my food. The cook, Amarantz—'

'Amarantz does not know you exist!' Sharn broke in. 'She thinks your trays are for an old palace servant who can no longer manage the stairs. And in any case I would trust her with my life. She would never serve the Shadow Lord.'

91

Marilen looked doubtful, but finally nodded. 'Then it must be one of the guards on this floor or the library floor,' she said. 'The guards must know that I am a special, secret visitor, for I never go downstairs.'

'But *they* do not go downstairs either, Marilen,' Sharn pointed out, her heart sinking as she realised how few the suspects actually were. 'Barda refused to risk them gossiping or being drugged, as happened once before. They are living on camping rations and sleeping in turns on this floor.'

Marilen shook her head in frustration. 'Then who can the spy be?' she demanded. 'Doom brought the tray to me. But Doom cannot be suspected. And nor can Josef, surely, though . . .' Her brow creased.

'What?' Sharn demanded. 'Tell me!'

'Josef was . . . different, in the library this morning,' Marilen said hesitantly. 'He looked cross and anxious. He rushed out, telling Ranesh to meet him in the kitchen to discuss an important matter. He has never done such a thing before.'

Sharn hesitated, unwelcome thoughts rushing through her mind.

'Marilen,' she said at last. 'Do not take this amiss, but I must know. You and Ranesh have become . . . good friends. Is it possible that you have given him a hint of the reason for your presence here?'

Marilen blushed to the roots of her hair. 'No, I have not!' she cried angrily. 'Ranesh knows I am of Tora, certainly, but anyone who looks at me must know that.

He has never asked why I am here, or what my future might hold, and I have never told him.' She lifted her chin defiantly. 'I have every reason not to do so!'

Those last words ringing in her ears, Sharn looked into the hurt, troubled eyes, and knew the girl was speaking the truth. She sighed, her heart very heavy.

'I am sorry to have caused you pain, Marilen,' she said quietly. 'But we must face the truth. Of all the suspects, Ranesh and Josef are the only ones who know you are here, and who were also present in the kitchen when your tray was being prepared.'

'Then however difficult it may be to believe, Josef must be guilty,' said Marilen in a hard voice.

'It cannot be Josef, Marilen,' whispered Sharn.

'Why not?' Marilen snapped, suddenly reminding Sharn vividly of Jasmine. 'Because he is old and frail? Because he says he saved *The Deltora Annals*? Surely we in Deltora have learned by now that wickedness can wear a smiling, deceiving mask?'

Indeed, thought Sharn, as they left the room of death, locking it after them. But I fear, Marilen, it is a lesson that your own heart has made you forget.

As they turned towards the stairway, they saw one of the library guards hurrying towards them. In his hand he held a folded sheet of paper, heavily sealed with wax.

'What are you doing away from your post, Follin?' Sharn asked sharply.

'It is my rest period, ma'am,' said the guard. He thrust the paper into her hand with an air of relief.

'The old fellow—the librarian—gave me this soon after you left the library with the young lady, ma'am,' he said, bowing distractedly in Marilen's direction. 'He said it had to be delivered to you urgently.'

Marilen stiffened. 'A message from Josef?' Sharn said faintly.

The guard nodded. 'He has been plaguing the life out of me ever since, ma'am, to carry it to you. But, as I told him again and again, I could not leave my post until my replacement came. Those were the orders, ma'am.'

He looked at Sharn anxiously, plainly worried that he had made the wrong decision.

'Quite right, Follin,' said Sharn, forcing a smile. 'Thank you. Go to your rest now. You have earned it.'

The guard made a clumsy bow, turned and lumbered away. With fingers that felt stiff and cold, Sharn broke the seal on the note and unfolded it.

> Madam,
>   When I saw you in the library just now—so kind and so brave—I realised that I could no longer keep silent. My heart is sorely troubled. I must speak to you at once. Do not delay, I beg you.
>   Your wretched servant,
> Josef

13 - Treachery

Sharn's heart was beating painfully as she ran up the stairs to the library. She dreaded hearing what Josef had to tell her.

Marilen was close beside her. Marilen had read the note also, and would not hear of being left behind. 'It could be a trap, Sharn,' she had said fiercely. 'You must not go alone! And in any case, I want to face him.'

There was no help for it. Whatever Josef had to say would have to be said in front of Marilen.

And perhaps it is for the best, Sharn thought despairingly.

She found Josef hovering by the library doors, watching for her under the stern gaze of the guards on duty. The old man's face crumpled in relief as he saw her approaching. And at the sight of Marilen, tears sprang into his eyes. He did not seem to notice how coldly the girl answered his greeting.

'I have set Ranesh a task on the other side of the

library,' he whispered, leading the two women through the huge, echoing room. 'I would prefer that he did not hear us.'

He ushered them into his own small chamber, and closed the door. His hands were trembling as he turned to face them. Plainly, now that the moment had arrived, he did not know how to begin.

'What is troubling you, Josef?' Sharn asked quietly, though her mind was boiling with fears.

Josef's mouth quivered. He took a deep breath. Then he said the last thing Sharn expected to hear.

'I have betrayed my trust,' he muttered. 'I let my pity for an old friend and protector sway me. And in doing so, I did great wrong.' He bowed his head in misery.

'Why, Josef! What do you mean?' exclaimed Sharn, very aware that Marilen was holding her breath.

'I wished only to comfort poor Amarantz. To tell her that Lief was sure to return to the palace,' whispered Josef. 'So—I wrote upon her slate that he would certainly return, that he *had* to return, because his Toran bride was here.'

Marilen made a strangled sound.

'*What*?' gasped Sharn, gripping the girl's arm.

Josef's eyes suddenly filled with tears. 'The message was only for Amarantz,' he choked. 'But then— suddenly—the giant, shaved-head woman, Lindal, burst into the room with the man, Jinks. They might have seen the message. I think they did.'

'Ranesh was in the kitchen too, Josef, was he not?' Sharn asked quickly.

'*Ranesh*?' Marilen's face was scarlet.

Josef looked confused and fearful. 'Do not blame Ranesh for concealing what I did, madam,' he cried. 'Ranesh knows nothing of it! I had wiped the slate clean by the time he arrived, and I did not tell him later. I was too ashamed, and fearful of his anger at my betrayal of our precious secret.'

He bowed his head. 'It is unforgivable,' he mumbled. 'Why, Lief himself entrusted us with the lady Marilen's care. He did not say who she was, of course. But the palace was buzzing with the news that he had gone to Tora for a bride, and naturally, when Ranesh and I met her, we put two and two together.'

'Naturally.' Sharn's head was spinning. Palace gossip. Of course! How could they have left this out of their calculations?

The blush had slowly faded from Marilen's cheeks, leaving her deathly pale. 'I am going to my bed chamber,' she said stiffly to Sharn. 'I have . . . tidying to do, as you may recall.'

She bowed shortly to Josef, and left the room, walking very quickly.

Josef looked after her with anguished eyes. 'Will she flee—back to Tora?' he whispered.

'Perhaps,' said Sharn slowly. 'She has had a great shock.'

'Ah, I would give anything to take back what I did!'

Joseph moaned. 'I have been in torment, in terrible fear that some harm would befall her. But that, at least, has not happened.'

Sharn made no reply. She was too occupied with her own thoughts.

'I am ready to go,' Josef added miserably.

Sharn looked up. Josef was standing before her, a small cloth bundle in his hand. For the first time she noticed that the little room had been stripped of every personal possession.

'Josef—' she began.

The old man hung his head. 'If you feel you can trust me not to disgrace myself again, I will return to my old home,' he mumbled. 'I would prefer it to a dungeon, though there is not much to choose between the two. But I will do whatever you—'

'Josef, do not be absurd!' cried Sharn. 'There is no question of your going away.'

He stared at her in disbelief

'No question!' Sharn repeated. 'You made a mistake, certainly. But surely we can all be allowed one slip?'

Josef's lips trembled. 'The results of my . . . slip . . . could be grave,' he said. 'The man Jinks—I do not think he can be trusted. And Lindal . . .'

'Jinks is dead,' said Sharn abruptly. 'Lindal is with Doom. There is only one person I must see to settle this.'

Josef gaped after her as she hurried out of the room.

✦

Sharn was panting when she reached the kitchen door.

She stood quite still for a moment, her hand on the knob, trying to calm herself. Then, to her surprise, she heard the muffled voice of Amarantz, and the sound of her own name.

'Sharn is upstairs, but she will be back at any moment. Wait here for her, I pray you. And try one or two of these, to please me. They are a new recipe. No doubt you are hungry from your journey.'

'Indeed we are,' boomed another voice—a voice Sharn knew well. 'I could eat my old horse, if we did not need him to pull the caravan. Come on, girl!'

There was a loud scraping of chairs.

Sharn threw open the door, taking in the scene in an instant. Two huge figures were sitting at the table. One was Doom's friend Steven, the strange Plains pedlar who had been such a good and powerful ally in the time of the Shadow Lord. The other—was Lindal!

And taking his place beside them was Doom himself, wearily pulling off his coat. But Sharn had no time, no space in her mind, to wonder why Doom and Lindal had returned, or how Steven had come to be with them. Her gaze was fixed on the platter towards which all three were reaching—a platter heaped with small, golden-brown cakes in silver paper cases.

'No!'

She sprang forward. As they shouted in shock, her arm crashed down on the table, sweeping the platter away from them. The platter fell to the floor, smashing on the stones, cakes bouncing and rolling away.

Amarantz, her face pale as parchment, fell to her knees, scrabbling to pick them up.

'Sharn! What is it?' roared Doom, astounded, almost angry.

Sharn could not answer. She was gasping, dizzy with relief. If she had been a moment later . . .

She steadied herself on the edge of the table and made herself look down at the old woman crawling on the stones of the kitchen floor.

Amarantz's eyes met hers. And suddenly it seemed to Sharn that something else was watching her from behind that familiar, faded blue. Something alien. Something cunning. Something wicked.

Her stomach churned with sickness. She shrank back, shivering.

And then, horribly, Amarantz began to laugh. 'Fools!' she cackled. 'Do you not know that you will never defeat me?'

With an oath, Doom leaped to his feet, his chair crashing behind him. Steven rose more slowly, gripping the edge of the table. The muscles of his arms and neck bulged as though he were lifting a great weight. He trembled all over. His eyes flickered from gold to brown as Nevets, the savage brother he carried within him, struggled for freedom.

'No!' Lindal ordered, putting a huge hand on his shoulder. 'Nevets, we do not need you here. Go back!'

The terrible shuddering quietened and ceased.

Shoulders heaving, Amarantz crouched toad-like,

watching them. 'What joy it would have been to have sent you the way of the poor little bride, Doom!' she croaked. 'And your friends, those ugly freaks of nature, with you. But, ah well, this feeble body is nearly worn out as it is. I will see you another time, Doom, in another place.'

She pressed her clenched fist to her mouth.

'Stop her!' Sharn exclaimed urgently.

Instantly understanding, Doom leaped forward.

But it was too late. The poisoned cake was already in the old woman's throat, and she was swallowing it whole.

'Soon we will be everywhere!' she hissed. 'Very soon . . .'

Her face changed, her eyes rolled back. With a terrible shriek she clutched at her stomach and fell sideways, her feet kicking, her head beating horribly against the stones.

As Doom, Lindal and Steven stood frozen with horror, Sharn ran to her. She could not help it. For whatever hideous force possessed the old woman, this was Amarantz, the friend of her youth. She could not let her die horribly, alone.

She took the jerking body in her arms and held it tightly. For a long moment there was no change. Then suddenly the eyes returned to normal. They stared at Sharn vacantly for a single moment, then seemed to focus.

'I am here, Amarantz,' Sharn whispered.

The eyes grew puzzled. The cracked lips opened. 'Sharn?' Amarantz murmured. 'Oh, Sharn, I had a terrible dream. Such a terrible dream.'

Sharn nodded, stroking the wet forehead, her eyes brimming with tears.

'I dreamed that the Grey Guards came to the pottery, and we were all taken,' sighed the old woman. 'And I—' Her eyes suddenly widened, filling with terror.

'Do not fear any more, Amarantz,' said Sharn quickly. 'The dream has ended now. Ended.'

'Yes.' The faded eyes grew peaceful once more. The lips curved in a half smile. And then the breathing stopped. For Amarantz, the nightmare had truly ended at last.

'What was that she said of "the poor little bride"?' asked Doom urgently.

'She thought she had poisoned Marilen. But she was wrong,' said Sharn.

She laid the old woman's head gently down and brushed the wisps of grey hair from the bloodstained cheek. Then she thought . . . she thought she saw something moving in the hair that trailed on the ground. Tears were blurring her eyes. She rubbed them, looked again, then jerked back with a scream of horror.

A long grey worm with a scarlet head was crawling from Amarantz's ear. It slithered out onto the floor in a trail of slime and writhed there, its tail lashing in fury.

14 - Leap of Faith

His face twisted in disgust, Doom strode forward and stamped on the evil thing, grinding it into the stones.

'What was it?' screeched Lindal.

'A new piece of Shadow Lord devilry,' Doom muttered. 'Amarantz was taken to the Shadowlands, it seems. And at some time—perhaps not long ago—*that* vile thing was put into her brain, and she was sent back.'

He looked down at Amarantz's crumpled body.

'At least we now understand what has been happening here,' he said. 'Why we are plagued by assassins and spies—all of them once good people.'

There was a short, fearful silence. One thought was in all their minds.

'There could be thousands of them,' said Lindal roughly, putting the thought into words at last.

'No.' Doom's brow was furrowed in thought. 'The words were, "*Soon* we will be everywhere". For some reason, the real invasion has not yet begun.'

'I think—I think that is because the process is not yet perfect.' Sharn was controlling the trembling in her voice with difficulty. 'It still causes . . . damage.'

As her companions stared, puzzled, she took a deep, shuddering breath.

'Do you not see?' she said. 'Amarantz said she had been deafened by a beating, but that was a lie. At the last, when she was herself again, when the worm had begun leaving her because it knew her time was ending, she could hear me clearly. The worm had been blocking her hearing, as well as controlling her mind.'

'Yes!' Doom's eyes blazed. 'And this explains many things. The babbling woman with the knife. The old guard who could not walk—'

'And—of course!—the man Pieter, who put the scorpion in Lief's bed chamber, was tormented by agonising headaches,' Sharn exclaimed. 'He was another—imperfect experiment.' Suddenly the horror was too much for her. She covered her eyes.

'The Shadow Lord is no doubt working to correct the fault in his process,' muttered Lindal. 'And when he is satisfied . . .'

'Ah, you are as gloomy as Nevets, girl!' growled Steven. 'Are you trying to make us lose all hope? I suspect you have a worm in your own painted skull.'

'My only headache is you, Steven!' Lindal retorted. 'I am simply being realistic. The Shadow Lord—'

She broke off as the kitchen door swung open.

Marilen walked in, her head high, colour burning in her cheeks. Her defiant eyes widened as she saw Doom, two huge strangers, and the body of Amarantz on the floor, but she did not hesitate. Ignoring everyone else, she spoke directly to Sharn.

'Please do not blame the guards because I am here. They had no orders to stop me. You all relied on my obedience for that. Well, I am tired of being obedient!'

'Marilen . . .' Sharn began, astonished. But Marilen had not finished.

'I came to tell you that, whatever you might think, I am certain that Ranesh is guilty of no wrong,' she said clearly. 'Also, that I am determined to stay here, whatever the future may hold. But I will no longer cringe upstairs in hiding and in ignorance of what is going on in the palace.'

Lindal snorted with laughter. 'Is this "the poor little bride"?' she whispered piercingly to Steven. 'She has grown a few muscles, it seems.'

Marilen's colour brightened even further but she tossed her head and turned to Doom. 'No blame will attach to you, or to Lief, if anything happens to me,' she said. 'This is my decision, and mine alone.'

'The decision is not yours to make, Marilen,' Doom said grimly. 'It is not only your father who fears for your safety.'

Marilen met his eyes without flinching. 'The decision *is* mine, Doom,' she said. 'I will be a prisoner no longer, and that is final!' She glanced at Steven and

Lindal, then looked back to Doom and lifted her chin. 'Discuss it with my father, if you wish,' she added, with an unmistakable air of triumph. 'He and Zeean are coming to Del.'

Sharn gave a muffled gasp. Steven and Lindal looked at her curiously,

'The letter came this morning,' Marilen said. 'I should have read it at once, but—' Again she glanced at Steven and Lindal. 'But something happened which drove it from my mind. Zeean and Father will be here in a day or two.'

'Well,' said Doom, his face unreadable. 'I am glad that I have returned in time to greet them.'

'Doom, why *have* you returned?' cried Sharn, suddenly recollecting.

'Lief and Barda are no longer in the Hills,' said Doom. 'They have followed Jasmine into the caverns under the earth.'

Sharn stared at him, joy and fear mingling on her face. 'Jinks *was* lying?' she gasped.

'Of course!' said Marilen quietly. 'Did I not tell you?'

'My mother's bees brought us the tale,' Steven put in. 'The story took time to spread to them, but it began, I gather, with vine-weaver birds in the Hills. I could not make head nor tail of it, for I had heard that Lief was in Tora. So I came to find out and, lo and behold, met Doom and Lindal on the road.'

'Under the earth . . .' Sharn shook her head. 'So Jasmine is truly trying to find a secret way to the

Shadowlands! And—and Lief and Barda are with her?'

'So it seems,' Steven nodded.

'But Doom, you must go after them!' cried Sharn. 'You must stop them! They cannot save the prisoners alone! All that will happen is that Lief will deliver himself—and the Belt of Deltora, Doom!—into the Shadow Lord's hands!'

'The Belt cannot be taken beyond Deltora's borders,' Doom said. 'We know this, and Lief knows it too.'

Sharn stared at him, unable to understand his calm. 'But what of the Pirran Pipe? Lief was so sure it was the only way to defeat the Shadow Lord on his own ground.'

'Perhaps Lief knows something we do not,' Marilen murmured.

'Perhaps he does,' said Doom. He looked at the girl thoughtfully for a moment, then turned back to Sharn. 'It was not an easy decision to return to Del, Sharn,' he said gently. 'My whole instinct was to continue. Then it came to me that it was Lief, Barda and Jasmine who restored the Belt of Deltora, and that they did it alone, without our help or protection.'

Sharn's eyes were blinded with tears. 'You are saying that we should trust them.'

'I am saying that we *must* trust them,' said Doom. 'Our place, our task, is here—especially now. All we can do is keep faith. And wish Lief, Barda and Jasmine well, wherever they may be.'

✦

Lief, Barda and Jasmine were in a place, and facing a

challenge, that not even Doom could have imagined. They were following Lief's plan. They were climbing the cavern wall that jutted beside the dome of Auron.

One of the raft-dwellers' old patched boats floated below them. The Piper himself sat in the stern. Penn was with him, looking up anxiously. At their feet lay what remained of a great coil of rope, slowly unravelling as the three companions made their perilous climb.

'The hand-holds are growing further and further apart,' gasped Barda, hauling himself up to a new ledge.

'You can stop now. We are already above the height of the dome,' said Jasmine, who was climbing nimbly above him, the rope trailing behind her. 'I will go on and attach the rope.'

She continued climbing, aiming for a lump of rock that jutted out high above them where the cavern wall curved to meet the roof.

Flattening himself against the rock beside Barda, Lief looked down. Far below, slightly to his right, the boat, small as a child's toy, rocked beside the band of seaweed. The great coil of rope had completely unravelled. Now the rope hung loosely down the rock face, its knotted end swinging, rising steadily as Jasmine climbed.

And looming before him, rising from sluggish, milky waters, was the rounded shape of the dimly glowing dome. Arach crawled in the shadowy filth heaped at its base, feeding, spinning, watching.

The sound of the Pirran Pipe rang in Lief's ears. He

closed his eyes, fighting it down.

'Very well. It is as secure as I can make it,' Jasmine hissed from above.

Lief looked up. Through the dimness he could see that Jasmine had pulled her end of the rope from her waist and looped it over the jutting rock, tying it firmly.

She tugged at the rope to test it. Then, without a sign of fear, she leaned back over the terrible drop, curved her body so her feet touched the rocky wall, and began running downward, the rope slipping through her hands.

In moments she had reached the ledge where Lief and Barda stood.

'Ready?' she asked casually.

Barda took hold of the rope, his hands gripping it firmly just below Jasmine's own.

'Promise me, Lief,' he muttered, 'that if this should go wrong, you will get back to the rafts and return to Del, however you are able. We cannot risk—'

'It will not go wrong if we follow Lief's plan,' snapped Jasmine. 'I am sure the rope is long enough, and the fastening will hold. The most important thing is to push off the cliff-face as hard as we possibly can, so that we swing out fast and far enough to cross the gap. And when I say jump, Barda, you must jump. At once!'

Barda gritted his teeth. 'And if I land safely on the top of the dome, but cannot hold myself in place?' he muttered.

'Then you will slide all the way down to the base

and fight Arachs,' said Jasmine calmly. 'But if not, you will simply wait while I return with Lief.'

There was nothing further for Barda to say. With a grim nod, he tightened his grip on the rope and bent one knee so that the sole of his boot was planted firmly against the cliff-face. Then, on the count of three, he and Jasmine launched themselves into space.

Lief held his breath as they swung in a great arc towards the dome, two small figures at the end of a rope that looked impossibly frail. Time seemed to stop. The milky sea crawled beneath them. Their shapes showed dark against the dome's dull glow, swinging up, up . . .

'Now!' shrieked Jasmine, and her voice echoed weirdly from the rock. *Now . . . Now . . . Now . . .*

Barda let go of the rope and sailed through the air. He landed on the dome flat on his belly. The surface of the dome shimmered but did not bend.

Jasmine was already swinging back, her small body hurtling towards the wall with terrifying speed. Lief stood ready to catch her, to cushion her so that she would not smash herself to pieces against the rock.

It was all over in seconds. In seconds, Jasmine was back on the ledge, gabbling instructions. In seconds, Lief was taking Barda's place, grasping the rope, pressing his foot against the wall, thrusting himself forward at Jasmine's signal.

Then he was flying, cold air rushing against his face, ears strained for Jasmine's call.

The dome was huge, filling his view. He felt himself

swinging upward. His brain filled with the singing of the Pipe. Louder. Louder . . .

'Now!' shrieked Jasmine.

Lief let go of the rope. His body sailed up through the empty air, up over the dome. His eye caught the flutter of Jasmine's clothing beside him. He could see Barda stretched motionless below.

Then he was falling. The dim glow of the dome rushed up to meet him. A warm, shimmering haze surrounded him.

He was aware of nothing but sound. Sweet, pure music poured through him, possessed him. It was blind instinct that made him reach for Jasmine's hand, clutch at Barda's shoulder, as he began to slip through the haze, and the magic of the Pirran Pipe drew him in.

15 - The Isle of Illusion

The grass was velvety soft under Lief's feet. Above his head arched a sky of perfect blue. Soft purple hills misted the horizon. The air was warm, and fragrant with the flowers that bloomed beside a rippling silver stream. The shadows under the trees were dappled with sunlight.

Pirra.

The birds seemed to sing the name. The stream babbled it. The leaves whispered it, rustling in a gentle breeze that seemed to breathe magic.

Lief felt hands tugging at his arm. Heard Jasmine's voice calling him from far away.

'Lief! Wake! We are inside the dome.'

The blue of the sky shimmered uncertainly, like water. The trees wavered.

'Lief, behind you! Look!' Jasmine's voice was sharp, urgent. It could no longer be ignored. Unwillingly, Lief turned.

A large crowd of people stood silently watching them. One, wearing the tall, stiff head-covering of a Piper, was dressed in purest white. The rest wore fluttering robes in soft, light colours. Many had flowers in their hair. They looked like the Aurons of the rafts, but they were taller, their faces were less sharp and their skin was golden brown.

And behind them, rising high above the tops of the tallest trees, seeming almost to touch the sky, was a glittering spire of glass. It flashed so brilliantly in the sunlight that at first Lief saw it only as a vast, shimmering column.

Then, as his eyes cleared, he realised that it had a shape. It was a vast statue of a woman—a Pirran woman, wearing the head-dress of a Piper. And he knew without doubt that the woman was Auron the Fair, who had long ago made music so beautiful that her audience wept.

The statue's long robe fell straight to the ground in a thousand glittering glass pleats as sharp as razors. Its fixed, unseeing eyes gazed serenely towards the purple hills. Its tall head-dress glared like a white flame against the blue sky. And embedded in the centre of the white flame, perfect and untouchable, was the stem of the Pirran Pipe.

Lief stared, aghast. No hands could have formed that vast image. It could only have been created by magic.

'No wonder we are here, in the centre of the island instead of at the edge as we expected,' Barda muttered.

'The mouthpiece of the Pipe pulled us to where it wanted us to be.'

'We will never climb that statue. We would be cut to ribbons in a moment if we tried,' Jasmine said. 'You will just have to persuade the dome-dwellers to give us the stem willingly, Lief. They look gentle enough. Surely they will listen to you.'

But Lief was silent, fighting despair. The statue had clearly been created to seal the stem of the Pipe away from every danger for eternity. Those who had made it would never willingly give up their prize. Never.

'Greetings, strangers.'

Lief forced his dazzled eyes downward, tried to focus on the figure standing before him. It was the man dressed in white. His arms were outstretched in welcome. The people behind him were also smiling, their robes fluttering like the petals of flowers ruffled by a gentle breeze.

'I am the Piper, Auris,' the man said. 'I cannot guess how you have come to our land, but know it must be for a good and beautiful purpose, since nothing evil can dwell here. On behalf of the people, I bid you welcome to Pirra.'

Welcome to *Pirra*?

Lief glanced at Barda and Jasmine. Both were struggling to keep their faces blank.

Auris was waiting courteously. Lief wet his dry lips. However hopeless this situation seemed, however sure he was that the dome-dwellers would be enraged by his request, and certainly would not grant it, he had to try.

'Thank you for your gracious welcome, Piper,' he said carefully. 'I am Lief, King of Deltora. I have come with my companions, Barda and Jasmine, to beg a favour of you.'

Auris's brow furrowed slightly, and it seemed to Lief that the sweet, sunny air flickered.

Then Auris's face cleared. 'Ah,' he said, bowing and smiling. 'Of course. Deltora. The realm beyond the mountains. You must forgive me, your majesty. For a moment the name escaped my memory. We of Pirra do not feel the need to travel. As I am sure you can well understand.'

He lifted an elegant hand, gesturing at the beauty around him.

'Indeed,' said Lief politely.

'A favour, you say?' Auris murmured.

Lief took a deep breath, glanced once again at Jasmine and Barda, willing them to be patient, and mentally crossed his fingers for luck.

'Many of our people are prisoners of the Shadow Lord, who is your enemy as well as ours,' he said, keeping his voice low and calm. 'The only thing that will save them is the Pirran Pipe, the stem of which you possess. We already have the mouthpiece, given to us willingly by the Plume people. This was how we were able to enter your magic dome so—'

'Stop!' The Piper's eyes had glazed. The people

behind him had begun flitting around so frantically that they seemed blurred. And the light—the light was flickering, dimming . . .

'There is no need to fear us!' Lief exclaimed hastily. 'We could not take the stem by force, even if we wished it. But I beg you will listen. We have journeyed far through the caverns, and faced many terrible dangers, to find your island.'

There was a low rumbling like distant thunder. The trees, grass and flowers quivered, then began to droop, as though their colours and shapes were melting into the trembling air.

Auris clapped his hands over his ears and screwed his eyes tightly shut. 'You are speaking gibberish! Your words have no meaning!' he shouted. He was breathing heavily. His face had turned as white as the belly of a fish. The crowd behind him was surging like a troubled sea.

'Do not listen to them! They are deluded fools!' he panted, plainly speaking as much to himself as to the people. 'There are no caverns. No dangers. No island. No dome. There is only Pirra, where all is beauty, all is peace, all is truth—'

'*You* are the one speaking gibberish, Piper!' Jasmine burst out, unable to keep silent any longer. 'There is *nothing* true in this place.'

'No!' Auris's eyes flew open and seemed to bulge in his head. 'Stop—'

The thundering sound grew louder. Lief looked

around him. Everywhere trees, flowers, grass and sky were shuddering, dissolving. Everything was melting, changing . . .

But . . . but this was not just a result of the Piper's anger, surely. This was something far more serious. It was as if . . . as if . . .

A terrible thought struck Lief, shaking him to his core. Suddenly he remembered the parchments Penn had shown him. He remembered the one thing that had puzzled him about them. He remembered Penn's anguished eyes, Penn's words:

I have done all you require of me, Piper, and it has cost me dearly

Yet what had Penn done but tell the history of her people's exile? Why had it cost her so dearly? Just because she feared for three strangers' lives?

Or because, in the telling, she had broken the law she held most sacred?

Truth is all-important.

What had Penn said when Barda asked her why her ancestors had been expelled from the dome?

They were dangerous . . . They were sick of pretence.

Dangerous? Why *dangerous*? Unless . . .

'You can make all the thunder and lightening you wish, Auris, but you *will* hear me!' Jasmine shouted. 'This is not Pirra! It is just an island protected by magic and filled with pictures. And you know that! I can hear it in your voice!'

There was a splitting, cracking sound, as though

117

the heavens themselves were breaking apart.

Auris shrieked.

And Lief's skin crawled as he understood at last. Penn had not lied. But she had not told the whole truth, either. And whatever the Piper claimed, Penn knew that this was the same as lying.

Auris and his people were swaying, backing towards the statue as though for protection. 'Foulness is in your mouth!' Auris howled at Jasmine. 'Your mind is crude, your heart is mean and shrivelled. You are a savage, whose eyes are not fit to see the beauty of Pirra!'

'Jasmine, do not answer! Let him be!' Lief cried urgently. 'Jasmine, the raft-dwellers *knew* this would happen. They are *using* us—to break the illusion and destroy the dome! The dome depends on belief! Doubt cracks it. Doubt will destroy it!'

But Jasmine was not listening to him. She was moving after Auris, shouting at him, beside herself with anger. 'I am not a savage, and *this is not Pirra!*' she shrieked. 'You pretend not to know that, but you do, you *do*! Outside this pretty dream of yours, there are monsters crawling and breeding in filth! There are caverns, and a great sea, and thousands of people who live in darkness because you—'

Thunder rolled and crashed above them.

'You have been sent by the unbelievers!' Auris screeched, his bulging eyes dark with terror. 'You are spies for all that is wicked and faithless! You have come to destroy me!'

And with that final word, the surging, fading crowd around him simply vanished, the flickering colours and shapes draining away into the grass like the phantoms they were.

Auris screamed—a scream of pure anguish that chilled Lief's blood.

'What has happened?' Barda roared over the cracking of the thunder. 'The people! Where have they gone?'

'They never were,' Lief shouted back, his stomach churning with horror. 'They . . . were part of the illusion. He is alone here. Who knows how long —'

'One by one the last of them failed me and died,' cried Auris. 'But I kept the faith! Alone I kept Pirra alive, harnessing the magic of thousands to keep its beauty perfect. Then you came. Spies and traitors! Saying what must never be said, speaking of things that must never be admitted—'

There was a flash of dazzling light and an ear-splitting crash. A jagged black crack opened in the sky, zig-zagging down to the trembling horizon like a bolt of lightning.

Auris shrieked and fell to the ground at the base of the statue. Desperately he stretched out his arms to it, his bony fingers clawing the air.

The split groaned and widened as the magic trapped for so long within the dome began escaping with rushing fury. Brilliant rainbow light could be seen through the gap as the cavern walls outside exploded into life, and colours dimmed for centuries gleamed.

Lief, Barda and Jasmine threw themselves to the ground, gripping the earth desperately as the force howled around them, tearing at the rags of trees, the faded tatters of flowers, grass, distant purple hills . . .

Then, suddenly, there was utter silence. But it was not the peaceful or exhausted silence of an ending. It was heavy and tense, as though everything was holding its breath. Waiting . . .

Cautiously, his skin prickling, Lief raised his head. The vision of Pirra had been swept away. Only the huge glass statue remained, rising into thick, still air which seemed to have been drained of colour. Auris lay face down at the statue's base, the tips of his fingers just touching the knife-like folds of the robe where they met the ground.

Everything was bathed in a weird half-light. The hills on the horizon had disappeared. Great branching clumps of fungus, tall and thick as ancient trees, hunched where trees once stood. Tiny ferns and mosses covered the clay and clustered along the banks of a deep and silent stream.

In the distance, the jagged tear in the fabric of the dome was now a gaping wound. At the top, it shone with rainbow light. But lower down it was deepest black.

That is strange, Lief thought slowly.

'Lief!'

Startled, Lief turned to see Barda scrambling to his feet and backing away to stand with his back to the nearest clump of fungus. Barda's eyes were fixed on the tear in the dome. Jasmine, too, was jumping up, reaching for her dagger.

'What—?' Lief began. Then he saw their faces change, and heard, behind him, a distant scratching, tearing sound.

He spun around. And realised why no light had been visible through the lower part of the hole in the dome. Something had been pressing against it. Something huge and black that was now ripping its way through the gap, leg by spiny leg.

Arach!

16 - Terror

With a low growl, the Arach forced itself fully through the gap in the dome. It rose on its back legs, huge, dwarfing the towering clumps of fungus that dotted the horizon.

It lurched forward abruptly, and to his horror Lief saw that another Arach was pushing through the gap behind it. Rainbows shone briefly through a tangle of black legs and a bloated body. Then the second Arach was through the hole, which was quickly blocked by a third.

'They are escaping from the light!' exclaimed Jasmine.

Of course! Lief thought. The Arach came from caves. They live and breed in dimness. They cannot bear bright light. Now that the caverns are lit by magic once more, the dome is the only place left for them to hide.

For the dome had not been brightened by the rainbow brilliance that shone behind the tear in its fabric.

It was as though the half-light that hung above the island stifled the brighter light, and prevented it from entering.

Five Arach now loomed on the horizon. And more were coming. The first arrivals had begun moving forward. Their massive bodies swaying on their long, spiny legs, they were feeling their way, moving awkwardly on the unfamiliar, solid ground.

'They are coming this way,' Jasmine exclaimed. 'Perhaps the statue attracts them. Or perhaps they can smell prey.'

'That is not a pleasant thought,' said Barda grimly. He looked thoughtfully at his sword. Large and heavy as it was, it seemed as small as a needle compared to the approaching beasts.

'We cannot fight them, Barda,' Lief muttered. 'Any more than we could fight the Sand Beasts in the Shifting Sands, or the Glus in the Maze of the Beast. We would not last a moment!'

'What else are we to do but stand and fight?' Jasmine hissed furiously. 'You have seen them run, Lief. They would catch us in an instant if we tried to flee! Are we just to lie down and wait for them to eat us?'

'We must hide,' said Lief. 'The light is poor. We must hide and hope they pass us by so that we can creep away.'

'Hide?' Jasmine exclaimed, looking around at the low ferns, the sparse clumps of fungus. 'There is nowhere to hide!'

Lief pulled off his cloak. 'There is,' he said. 'Just as

there was, not long ago, in the River Broad when an Ak-Baba was overhead. Just as there was in the Shifting Sands when Grey Guards were approaching. Have you forgotten so soon?'

Jasmine's green eyes flashed. 'I have forgotten nothing,' she said abruptly. 'I thought you had, however.'

Lief stared at her, hurt and confused. He could not understand her meaning.

Barda cleared his throat. 'If we are to hide, we should do so at once,' he said. 'The creatures are moving slowly, but their strides are huge. They will be upon us very soon. What of Auris?'

Lief tore his eyes away from Jasmine's and glanced over to where Auris lay beside the statue. He thrust the cloak into Barda's hands. 'You and Jasmine take cover,' he said. 'If he still lives, I will fetch him.'

'Keep low! Take care!' Jasmine called softly after him as he began to run.

Obediently, Lief lowered his head. At least she cares whether I live or die, he thought. But why did she say that, about my forgetting our quest for the Belt? How could I ever forget?

Auris was rigidly still, and his eyes were closed. But as Lief drew near enough to the statue to feel its strange, radiating warmth on his skin, he realised that the last of the dome-dwellers was not dead, or even unconscious.

Auris was chanting under his breath—so softly and rapidly that Lief could not catch the words.

'Auris,' Lief urged, touching his arm. 'Auris—come with me. There is danger here.'

Auris screwed his eyes more tightly shut, but made no other sign that he had heard. He did not lift his head, or move his fingers from the hem of the statue's robe. Did not stop, for a moment, his frenzied whispering.

Lief glanced nervously at the approaching Arach. The creatures were closer now. There were at least ten of them, crawling in a wedge-shaped pack with the first, and largest, in the lead.

'Auris!' he said sharply. He tried to pull the Piper away from the statue, but the thin fingers immediately clutched at the razor-sharp glass and gripped it tightly. Blood ran in streams into the ground, but still the whispering voice did not pause.

Lief bent closer, straining to hear.

'Thespellmustholdthespellmustholdthespell . . .'

One phrase, endlessly repeated.

'Lief!' Barda and Jasmine were beckoning urgently from behind the fungus where they had taken cover. Lief could hardly see them. As always, his cloak had taken on the colour of its surroundings. It was disguising them perfectly.

He turned and was shocked to see how close the Arach were, how far they had crawled in just a few moments. They had quickly become used to the solid earth under their feet. They were moving steadily, confidently.

They still had not seen him. But any moment . . .

Desperately, hissing warnings and commands, Lief tried again to drag Auris free. But the Piper's bleeding fingers gripped the warm glass like steel bands, and his babbling chant did not cease.

It was no use. In despair, Lief left him and crawled to where Jasmine and Barda crouched anxiously waiting.

'He will not move,' he said, creeping under the cover of the cloak with them.

'It is his choice,' Jasmine answered calmly. 'Perhaps he thinks the magic of the statue will offer more protection than a hiding place.'

Lief shook his head. He had a lump in his throat which made it hard to speak. 'I do not think so,' he said. 'I think he is using the last of his power, and the power of the Pipe, to try to hold onto all that remains of his world.'

He had a sour, burning taste in his mouth—the taste of defeat, anger and guilt. He thought of Penn and the Piper. Were they still watching from their boat beyond the seaweed band? Or were they already hastening back to the rafts, delirious with joy because they had regained for their people the light and magic so long denied them?

'For all the Piper of the rafts knew, there were thousands of people inside the dome,' he muttered, his eyes on the approaching Arach. 'Thousands, whose lives would have been destroyed by what he did. By what *we* did, in ignorance.'

'He was fighting for the lives of his own people,' said Barda in a low voice. 'Like any good commander, he seized a chance for victory when it came.'

Lief thought of the Piper's glowing eyes as he spoke to Penn about the visitors.

They could be our salvation.

'And like any good commander,' Barda went on, even more quietly, 'he knew that sacrifices would have to be made in the cause. Unfortunately, *we* seem to be the sacrifices in this case. The beasts are not going to pass us by.'

The Arach were almost upon them. They had slowed as they neared the statue, and now they had stopped completely.

'It is the warmth,' breathed Jasmine. 'They stayed close beside the dome not just because of the food, but because it was warm. They like the statue for the same reason. They will probably try to nest around it.'

Lief felt sick. Was it so? Were they condemned to crouch here, with no chance of escape, helplessly watching the slaughter of Auris? Knowing that the second part of the Pirran Pipe was lost forever because of something they themselves had done?

He watched with horrified fascination as the largest of the Arach moved closer to Auris's motionless body.

The creature was gigantic. Monstrous. Its eyes bulged from its glossy black shell, gleaming red. Its fangs slowly opened and closed, dripping venom.

Its two front legs reached out delicately, took Auris in their grip, and tugged. Auris's hands tightened on the glass. He did not stir.

'No!' Lief whispered in agony. He tensed himself to rise.

Barda's hand clamped firmly on his wrist. 'Be still! We cannot help him! There is still a chance we can get you out, Lief. You, at least.'

'That is not important any more,' Lief hissed back. 'All that matters is—'

But at that moment, the Arach lost patience. With a low growl, it tore Auris away from the statue, and lifted him high into the air.

Auris's shriek of terror and despair chilled Lief to the bone. Cold sweat broke out on his brow, and he began shivering violently. He wanted to cover his ears, but his hands were rigid. He wanted to look away, but he could not move.

The beast rose on its hind legs and pulled its victim closer. Auris screamed and screamed again, writhing in an agony of fear. The monster's red eyes watched him closely, almost as if it was enjoying his terror. Then suddenly its fangs lunged forward and sank into his neck, mercifully ending his struggles.

The spiny, clawed legs instantly began tearing the limp body apart, shredding it exactly as they had shredded the boat.

The other Arach closed in, scrabbling for a share of the prize, fighting over every dripping scrap of flesh that fell from their leader's jaws.

Sickened, Lief at last managed to look away.

And only then did he see what had been right in

front of his eyes since the moment Auris was plucked into the air.

The statue's arms were rising. As Lief watched, astounded, the hands covered the serene face. Then—suddenly—the glass was no longer clear and gleaming. It had become thick white.

Lief pressed his hand over his mouth to stifle a cry. Glancing sideways, he saw that Jasmine and Barda were also staring in amazement.

There was a strange, grating sound. Then, with no further warning, the statue simply crumbled, collapsing in an ear-splitting, thunderous shower of shattered glass.

'Beware!' Lief shouted, pulling Barda and Jasmine with him to the ground.

They lay there under the cloak, eyes tightly closed as jagged fragments sprayed upwards, then fell again, pelting the ground like deadly hail. They heard the Arach bellowing, the cracking sound as shooting glass cracked the beasts' shells like darts.

And then, at last, all was still once more. Cautiously Lief lifted his head. His mind filled, echoing, with the sound of the Pirran Pipe. The Pipe's stem was there, somewhere, buried deep in shattered glass. It called to him, beckoned him. But he held himself rigidly, knowing he could not stir.

The two Arach which had been closest to the statue lay where they had fallen, their legs kicking and tangling uselessly. But the others, despite small cuts and cracks in their shells, had been injured only enough to drive them into a fury. Growling they rose onto their back legs, their front legs pawing at the air.

Barda cursed under his breath.

But Jasmine was looking up. 'The dome,' she said softly. 'The dome . . .'

There was a low, sighing sound. And then the dome—simply melted away, disappearing like mist.

The light was blinding, filled with rainbows, glittering, dazzling. Lief, Barda and Jasmine buried their faces in their arms. The Arach shrieked and scurried frantically away, leaving their two injured fellows to die where they lay.

And Penn, standing panting in the place which once had been the gap in the dome, a bone spear clutched awkwardly in her hand, sobbed part in frustration, part in relief, for there was nothing, now, for her to do.

17 - Peace

Much later, in Penn's little hut on the rafts, all was the picture of peace. Light streamed through the window, bringing with it the sounds of rejoicing. Tresk and Mesk bobbed lazily in their bowl. Kree, cradled in Jasmine's arm, cautiously tested his healing wing.

Lief, Barda and Jasmine sat around the stove with Penn and the Piper, the cheers of the raft-dweller crowds ringing in their ears. A huge platter of Molisk patties and a basket of warm bread lay between them. Filli sat on Jasmine's shoulder, nibbling sea berries which made his tiny nose wrinkle with surprise and pleasure.

Even Fury and Flash lay quietly in their cages, side by side. Their adventure with the Arach seemed to have changed their minds about the wisdom of fighting. Together they had faced a terrible enemy, a spider far mightier than either of them could ever have imagined. For now, they had decided that peace was a blessing.

'So. The Arachs have gone back to the caves where they came from,' the Piper said, biting into a patty with relish. 'They could not bear the light and the cold. I told you, Penn, that it would be so.'

Penn glanced at Lief, Barda and Jasmine. Her food lay untasted on its plate. She, at least, was still not at peace.

It would be a relief to her, Lief knew, if the matter hanging between them was put into words.

He was very aware that the stem of the Pirran Pipe, retrieved from the pile of shattered glass on the Isle of Auron, was at this very moment firmly tucked inside the Piper's robe. He knew it would not be wise to anger the Piper now.

But he had to speak his mind, for all their sakes.

'You used us, Piper,' he said. 'We suspected that you were using us as tools to obtain the stem of the Pirran Pipe. But you were doing much more than that. You were using us as a weapon to destroy the dome.'

'To destroy the thing that was sucking the life from my people?' the Piper said mildly, licking his fingers. 'Yes, I did. Would you not do the same for Deltora?'

Lief hesitated.

'Of course you would, Lief,' Jasmine said sharply. 'You can be cold and calculating enough when you believe the good of the kingdom requires it.'

'What do you mean, Jasmine?' Lief exclaimed, startled by the sudden, bitter note in her voice.

Jasmine shrugged. 'If you think a secret should be

kept, for example, you keep it,' she said shortly. 'Even from those it most concerns.'

She looked down at her hands to avoid Lief's eyes. She was furious with herself. She had not meant to speak so rashly.

She had tried not to think of Faith, the little sister who was a prisoner in the Shadowlands and who Lief had tried to prevent her from discovering. She had tried not to think of the high-born Toran girl Lief had brought in secret to the palace to become his queen.

Most of the time she was successful. But now and again she remembered, and the knowledge jabbed at her heart like a spear, making her lash out in anger and pain.

Lief felt his face grow hot. He remembered Jasmine's hasty words on the island.

I have forgotten nothing . . . I thought you had, however.

Was it possible that Jasmine had guessed the secret he had kept at such cost to himself? The secret that was like a crushing burden?

No, surely not. He and Doom had been so careful!

He glanced at Barda. But Barda had turned to look out the window, as though there was something of great interest happening on the silent street.

Jasmine simply suspects there *is* a secret, Lief told himself. She feels the barrier that hidden knowledge always creates between two people who have always spoken the truth to one another.

Lief felt it himself, and he hated it. He longed to

tear the barrier down. To end the terrible, aching loneliness it made him feel at moments like this.

But he knew he could not. Not until all was safe. Not until Deltora's future had been secured.

He became aware that the Piper was regarding him curiously, and his blush deepened.

'It is sometimes necessary for leaders to do things they would prefer not to do,' the Piper said, as though he was speaking to himself. 'Sometimes they have to put aside their own wishes, even their own deepest longings, for the greater good of all. It is ... not pleasant. Especially when their actions anger those they care about.'

Jasmine did not raise her head. But Lief could see that she had heard. He prayed that she had also understood.

'You think, no doubt, that I am evil,' the Piper went on, in the same even tone. 'You think Penn tricked you, on my orders. You think I used you as tools to destroy the dome. You think that I cared nothing for your lives, or the lives of the people who may have lived on the island.'

'It did occur to us,' said Barda dryly.

The Piper shrugged his narrow shoulders. 'It is true that I forced poor Penn to do what she did,' he said, glancing at the history-keeper, who had bowed her head. 'She was sorely distressed by the task. Like all raft-dwellers she respects truth above everything else. I suggested that she let you *read* our history, so she would not have to tell it.'

'But the history was not complete,' said Lief. 'The two parchments Penn gave us were torn, the first at the bottom, the second at the top. They were once part of the same document, I think. You tore a section from the middle before giving the story to us. Is that not so?'

Penn nodded miserably. Without speaking, she crawled to her feet and went over to the hanging baskets. She slid a fragment of parchment from the back of one of them, returned to the stove and thrust the scrap into Lief's hand.

The dome could only remain whole, however, while all within it believed in the illusion, and shut out any doubting thoughts. Because they denied that the island was Pirra, and spoke aloud of the caverns and the dome, our ancestors continually threatened the dome's existence.

'If I had allowed Penn to show you the whole parchment, would you have helped us?' the Piper asked, turning his cold little eyes on Lief.

Lief hesitated. 'We needed the second part of the Pirran Pipe,' he said finally. 'We would have entered the dome, even if the truth was known to us.'

'Perhaps,' agreed the Piper. 'But perhaps you would have been so careful in what you said that the dome would have remained closed, and my people would have continued to live in growing darkness. I could not take that risk.'

He sighed. 'So I am guilty of the first charge you

have laid at my feet. But I am not guilty of the others.'

He took some bread from the basket and bit into it. 'I knew the dome-dwellers would not harm you, for blood may not be spilled inside the dome,' he said thoughtfully, with his mouth full. 'And I did not think that you or anyone else would have to face the Arach. I thought the dome would shatter, the light would return to the caverns, and the Arach would flee to the dimness of the caves at once.'

'But that did not happen,' said Barda gruffly. 'Auris kept the spell alive. He held the dome, damaged as it was, in place with all the force of his will. Only his death ended it.'

'Indeed.' The Piper shrugged. 'I had not counted on that. But as soon as we realised what had happened, Penn and I called the guards. Then we entered the dome ourselves, even before the guards arrived, to do what we could to aid you.'

He took another bite of the bread, and glanced at Penn. 'What use we could have been, I do not know,' he said, chewing. 'As I told Penn, we were almost certainly going to our deaths. But she insisted. Fortunately, the man Auris expired in time to save us all.'

Lief shuddered as a vision of Auris's terrible death rose before his eyes. He glanced at the Piper with dislike, then looked away, repelled by his coldness.

And yet, he thought . . . for all his seemingly uncaring words, the Piper *had* entered the dome. *Had* put his own life at risk.

Lief looked again at the small, wrinkled Auron, who was chewing his bread with every appearance of enjoyment. Whatever he pretended, the Piper was not without feeling. Not without honour or courage. He was just a being who preferred to keep his emotions locked within himself. It was his way of surviving.

'We never dreamed there would be just one soul left on the island,' Penn burst out, breaking her silence at last. 'We knew there would not be a large number, however. The dome-dweller colony could never have thrived. Fewer and fewer children were being born to the tribe, even at the time our ancestors left it.'

The Piper nodded, swallowing. 'Children are not good at living a lie. Children have too much energy, are too impatient, and ask too many questions,' he said.

He glanced slyly at Jasmine. 'Some people, indeed, keep these qualities long past the age of childhood,' he added. 'That, I think, is a good thing. But it is not always comfortable for those who love them.'

In the tense silence that followed, he calmly finished eating. Then he brushed the crumbs from his hands, and fumbled in the folds of his robe.

'Here is the stem of the Pirran Pipe,' he said, drawing out a small piece of carved wood and handing it casually to Lief. 'Use it as you will. We would be glad to have it back when you have achieved your aim, but for now we can do without it.'

Lief took the stem of the Pipe in trembling hands. As he touched it, his whole body tingled, and the Pipe's music rang in his ears. He took the mouthpiece from the inside pocket of his shirt, and screwed the two pieces together.

'Thank you,' he managed to say.

The Piper allowed himself a small smile. 'You are welcome,' he said. 'In fact, it is no great sacrifice. After all, we have done without our part of the Pirran Pipe for a very long time. For now, the magic that lives in every Auron, and which has now been returned to us, will be more than enough. Thanks to you, the island is ours once again. What more can we ask?'

The music in Lief's mind rose and fell, sweet and filled with longing. He looked up at Barda and Jasmine. He saw their eyes fixed on the magical object in his hands, and knew that they too could feel its power.

One more effort . . . one more adventure, and the Pirran Pipe would be complete.

And then?

And then, thought Lief, we will be ready. Then we can go, for good or ill, to the Shadowlands.